I0734729

iii

JUSTIFYING SOUND STRIDER
Landscapes of Mercy, Book 3
By Cindy Amos

Cindy M. Amos

Dedicated to the original Fearing clan
My cousins Anna Joyce (Fearing) McPherson
and Linda Dale (Fearing) McClintock
who ran barefoot up the path to the Fearing
Cottage with me
once upon a time ago

My deliverance approaches;
My salvation extends to the rim;
Those who dwell on the shoreline's edge
shall put their hope in me.
On My arm alone they will rely.
Isaiah 51:5

The author would like to acknowledge the following for their support and encouragement with this book:
Cover photo of Roanoke Sound from Getty Images
Pamela Bower, Proofreader
Janice Fairbairn, Marketing Strategist for LOM Series Members of South Central Kansas ACFW Chapter
Cynthia Hickey of Forget Me Not Romances
& Inspiration of the Holy Spirit

LANDSCAPES OF MERCY SERIES BOOK
THREE

Yet there is one ray of hope:
God's compassion never ends.
Only the Lord's mercies have kept us
from complete destruction.
Great is His faithfulness;
His lovingkindness renews each day.

Chapter 1

Tourists clogged the main artery of the Outer Banks and seemed to push the island toward its tipping point. Marin Evans sulked all the way up from Whalebone Junction heading to Milepost 13, where she would arrive over half an hour late for her interview. Warned that the native in her scopes could be a tad on the temperamental side, she worried that the article would be a total washout just because she hadn't allowed enough transit time. She swallowed the catty chastisement that came to mind for the tourists and defaulted to a quick prayer instead.

Hired in March as the executive director for a new nonprofit coalition, her mission aimed at unifying several strong forces in the community. So far, it proved to be a challenge to balance the pride of key players while she slipped subtle suggestions for ways things could be improved into the conversation. Who knew that the outer rim of a nation comprised of sand and sun could be so resistant to change? She might as well walk straight up Jockey's Ridge every day, an easier task than the delicate negotiation between such hardheaded factions.

The sign for Soundside Road came up on her left so she dropped the turn signal and immediately drew the wrath of the driver behind her when she slowed. A glimpse in the mirror revealed a New England license plate and she rolled down her window to add a straight-armed hand signal for the left turn. That generated a not-so-nice reciprocative gesture from the irate driver behind her car. Traffic lagged in the opposite lane and she made a hasty swerve for the crossing. Empty, Soundside Road unfolded ahead in tranquil contrast to the beach bypass road.

The embayment of Roanoke Sound soon appeared as a band of water across the lower half of her windshield. Now late afternoon, the sun had lowered on the western horizon leaving a serene shimmer on its smooth surface. She slowed to enjoy the scenery as hummocks of wax myrtles blocked signs of development further south. Finally, only a row of waterfront cottages remained, and the road hooked sharply left at the water's edge.

Her destination held the distinction of being historically significant, despite its pending doom. When she glanced ahead, she spotted its towering eminence, a wood planked cottage made bric-a-brac with the plastering of ship nameplates all over its weathered exterior. The dashboard accentuated the fact that she was arriving thirty-five minutes late for the interview. Her stomach tensed even after she parked and stepped out of the car.

A path of concrete stepping stones dotted the way to a massive front porch, which seemed to wrap around the entire structure. No doubt a grand dame in its time, the sag of deterioration now evidenced itself on every horizontal surface. In a dozen bounds she stood at the front door, banging a brass ship's anchor against the splintered wood. No response came.

She wandered around half the porch, reading the nameplates and momentarily forgetting her mission. The historical society and the recreation agency disagreed over proper use for the soon-to-be-available resource here which placed her in the role of mediator. From the vantage point of the porch, she scanned the property and understood the reason for the one-upmanship.

Native flowers winked from the unkempt sandy yard which flowed around the cavernous house and down to the sound. She spied a man down by the water's edge preparing to go out on the sound and decided to make contact with him for possible leads. She'd gain access to the persnickety owner one way or another.

After a quick snapshot of the house, Marin secured the camera and broke into a trot. Having returned to the edge of the road for his white bucket, the waterman seemed seconds from disappearing onto the openness of the sound. Her heart stirred at the authenticity of the setting and she wondered how long men with salt in their veins had plied these waters for a living. She snapped another photo and felt a surge of bravery.

"Excuse me, I don't mean to keep you but I'm looking for the owner of the Fearing Cottage." Winded from the run down, she braced her hands against her knees.

A guy about her age loaded a bucket and pulled a

line from the sandy shore like he hadn't heard her at all. He tugged his hat down. "You're not keeping me. That sun is going to set in less than two hours and I have crab pots to check." The end of the line revealed an anchor that had been hiding in the tall grass along the shoreline. He splashed the spiked metal into the lapping waters of the sound, cleaned the sand off, and lowered it over the side of a small rowboat.

When he turned back to her, the desperate attempt to salvage her interview bottomed out to nothing. "Tyde Fearing—do you know him?" She tried not to let the exasperation seethe its way into her tone. "I'm Marin Evans with the Dare County Advocates and I had an appointment to interview him at five-thirty for the Sunday issue of the Daily Advance."

He stepped into the boat. "Looks like time isn't on your side either. That was over half an hour ago." With the shove of his last step, the little boat began to float away. He grabbed the oars on either side and made the boat face her as though to finish her off.

Steamed by her predicament, the late May heat became even less comfortable. "Right. Thanks to tourist season the island's arteries have clogged, which left the causeway impassable. That's my fault for being a gringo and not realizing the difference vacation season would make. I've only lived here a couple of months." She bit her lip thinking she might have struck a soft spot with her confession.

He tilted his head to clear his line of vision under the hat brim. "I'm Tyde Fearing and I waited for you as long as I could. Guess we'll have to do the interview some other time."

His difficult reputation seemed to play out in front

of her. A phantom of her deadline popped into her head. Marin knew the peacemaking between the warring factions couldn't wait either. "What if you let me come with you?" She posted her hands on her hips like sails. Seconds passed with only waves lapping the shoreline and her heartbeat echoing her novice plea. The word "grace" flashed into her thoughts and she claimed it as the boat bobbed across a shore-bound wake.

A growl echoed up his throat. "Come on out." He dug the oars in the shallow bottom.

Relieved, she flashed a smile and wiggled her sandals off into the grass. With a splash, she welcomed the waters and a chance to make amends. "Thanks. You won't regret this." She deepened her smile to let him know she really meant it. As she waded out, she read the boat's name off the bow and wondered what a water strider was.

~

Tyde steadied the boat as a feminine foot with blue toenails appeared over the gunwale. *I must be absolutely insane.* The insistent blond stumbled at the point of being half in and half out, so he reached over to lend support. Taut and tanned, her arms came to him accompanied by the scent of coconut. Water dripped in as her second foot made the journey on board. She crouched, looking lost at sea.

He shoved an overturned bucket into the bow with his free hand. "You'll have to sit forward to center our weight. It's a small boat and I don't usually have company." The understatement of the year, he'd *never* had company out on his rounds, but she didn't need to know that for her interview. A notepad bulged from her back pocket as she steadied a camera in her hand. "Oh, water can be brutal on digital devices. Maybe you should stow it away before your next casualty occurs.”

“No need. I paid extra to get the waterproof model once I knew where my new job would take me.” She settled the bucket evenly off the bow ribs and took a seat.

“So you do plan ahead for some things.” He took a power stroke with the oars.

“Should I operate one of those?” She reached for an oar.

“Absolutely not. I don’t have time to go in circles today. You stick to the interviewing and I’ll stick to my crab pots, but thanks anyway.”

She withdrew further into the bow. “Before we get to my questions, do you want to lend me some wisdom for handling tourist season?”

An irreverent laugh erupted as he buried the oars without a splash. The boat shoved forward and he felt light, like being freed from some indescribable weight. “Tourist season holds a double-edged sword that vexes the locals, but gives us enough income to last out the year. I can’t bite the hand that feeds me, as these crabs are destined for my buddy’s seafood restaurant. That payback floats my bills.”

A generous smile wiggled her sunglasses as she stretched her legs out between them.

Caught off guard, the feminine display really worked on him, so he took a power stroke to offset the unexpected emotional surge.

“I’ve got to learn to balance my appreciation of the Outer Banks with respect for the people who come over to enjoy the same things I love,” she admitted. “Originally from Elizabeth City, I’ve vacationed here all my life, but living in Manteo now makes me appreciate the natural beauty of the islands even more."

"Whereabouts in Manteo?" The question leaked out before he could prevent it. Now she would think he was interested. He spied the first cork float off the port bow and stroked with his right oar.

She glanced over her shoulder and her blunt cut hair cascaded toward him in a wave. "I live in a tiny gatekeeper's cottage once part of Andy Griffith's estate." She looked over her dark glasses at him. "I'm renting now, but it might come up for sale by the end of summer. I'm saving my pennies but when you work for a non-profit, all you make is pennies."

The flash of her sky-hued eyes leaked into his comfort zone like cool liquid. "Try living by crustaceans. At least blue crabs are in demand. Jimbo pays me pretty well. He sticks it to the tourists after he runs the crabs through a pot of hot water. Don't know what I'll do once they evict me off the sound side, though."

"Want to talk about the Fearing Cottage now?" A hint of tenderness tempered her voice. Her eyebrows arched above the rim of her sunglasses.

He knew he couldn't avoid her interview questions forever. A float thumped against the bow and he pushed back with the oars. "Let me get this first pot in. Switch places with me. I'm going to need that bucket."

"Okay by me." She rose in a stoop and steadied herself on the gunwale.

He departed the stern bench the moment she alighted only to chastise himself for not lingering in her coconut scent zone for a few more seconds. Too bad he acted all business, even when it didn't pay off. Old habits die hard on the water, and being out here to merely recreate lingered like a far-off dream.

He took the cork float in his hands. "Try to steady the boat as I lean out and haul this pot in," He hiked out over the gunwale, the boat against his ribs as she countered his weight with even measure. Hand over hand, he brought the trap line up and suddenly the horizon teemed with life. In fluid motion, he swiveled and banged the trap down over the bucket. The first of four crabs dropped out. He unpinned the wired hinge and dumped the remaining captives.

Marin leaned over the bucket opposite him and came up whistling."Blue crabs?" A blank notepad bobbed in her hand.

"Yep. These are all big enough to keep. I put the undersized soft-shelled ones back and let them grow up a little. Four captives might be a slow start to the four dozen I'd like to haul in today. Memorial weekend's here, which means demand will be up at Jimbo's."

She positioned the notepad front and center. "Well, I'd better get cranking with my article while the crustacean crowd is thin."

His reflexive moan must have come out more audible than he'd intended.

She peered over her glasses again. "This would be a little less painful if you just talked about the situation and let me record it from your perspective."

Dropping the trap, he retook possession of the oars and motioned her to one side to share the bench with her. "Okay, here goes. Once upon a time there was an islander who didn't care for the oceanfront, so he built a humble cottage along the sound side and set down roots in a less hostile environment, away from the crash of the surf and the angry sea."

"I like this story." Dimples appeared on her round face. "Who would that man be?"

From close range, those dimples possessed a lethal draw. Tyde pulled the oars toward the next float on the horizon as if to shove their effect aside. "He was my great-grandfather, Willis Jarvis Fearing. His people were from deep on the island, down Buxton way. Have you ever heard anyone talk from Buxton? They've got the deepest drawl you could ever imagine."

Her curiosity seemed to get riled as she squirmed on the bench. "No, can't say that I have. Give me a sample of the colloquial lingo and let me process it."

"Here's how my dad taught it to me. 'It's hoi toide on the sound soide.'" He laughed for punctuation. When she laughed with him and reached for the right oar, it broke his rhythm and heated his neck. He struggled to regain his stroke.

She detached her grip."You have a great name, Tyde, so fitting for your life here." Her tone held the velvet smoothness of admiration.

He looked out over the water and lost his train of thought. After a few seconds, she cleared her throat and he realized she might be waiting for the rest of the story. The second cork struck the bow and when he made his way forward, she took the oars. This time the wet line seemed comforting in its familiarity, not an interruption. "Your name sounds like 'mariner.' Does that make you seafaring stock?"

"Yeah, sort of, as Marin means 'from the sea.' I don't know where my mom got the idea, except she admitted being tired of that landlocked feeling."

"I couldn't be a mainlander." Water dripped down

his elbows as he lifted out the trap. "Water has to break the horizon for me, but I prefer the back side of the islands like my great-grandfather." A quick count revealed this load brought double the last yield, and a smile hooked into his cheeks. Her hands reached over to unwire the hinge and he shook the box once she had it released, dropping the crabs into the bucket with a clatter.

She peered over the bucket rim. "It looks like they're fighting."

He tossed the reset trap in and slid back to the stern, taking the oars. With a hard pull, they were off to the third trap. "Good. Keeps them busy," he quipped, eyeing her scribbled notes.

"But not out of trouble."

"Too late for that now, isn't it?" His tone carried more than a hint of insinuation. With a woman in his boat, maybe he was the shellfish out of water. *The problem with making exceptions to your rules was that somebody always wiggled their way in.*

"Back to the story of Fearing Cottage," she replied, business-like despite the breach.

~

The sand felt solid and warm under her bare feet as she left the sound. Too bad she had to go. She watched the wiry-haired waterman tend his boat a few seconds longer than intended. "Thank you so much for the lovely float—and for taking my questions." She retrieved her sandals to break the tension riding her departure. "Check out the article in the Sunday paper. I hope you'll enjoy it."

Tyde stowed the oars and pitched the anchor line into the grass. As he stepped ashore with the teeming bucket in hand, his tanned face grew taut as though he was having some inner turmoil. After a few seconds, he looked her in the eyes. "I'm down here every day. Come back sometime—without the notepad. Looks like you're a crab magnet." He winked to convince her.

It came across like an open invitation to return for personal reasons, but Marin couldn't quite be sure. Though appealing on the surface, how might his offer fit against the reputation of being a tad temperamental? She crossed the high water mark to head back so she could write the article, though part of her didn't want to leave.

Chapter 2

Marin took the trash out and lamented the beauty of the midday from her back stoop. She'd been at it all morning and had reached the breaking point with housework. "No one should spend Memorial Monday cleaning house all day."

She stepped out to the side of the cottage and caught a glimpse of Roanoke Sound. It happened to be the far side of the waters she had plied in the little boat named Water Strider. The man behind the oars came to mind, the same thoughts that had distracted her while writing the article. That she had found him remarkable, like some relic from the past living tucked away from modern life, seemed of little consequence. At least, that's what she kept telling herself. A colorful sailboard skimmed by and she watched the effortless beauty of how it graced the water.

With the Fearing cottage article behind her, the first skirmish loomed on the horizon. She had until the end of June to find a compromise between the historical society's claim for preservation of at least part of the antiquities and the recreation department's greedy quest for water access. Not a land use guru, she did have a knack for compromise. Her proposal would have to bring to bear the best of both worlds, as neither of the warring agencies possessed a penchant for balance. Not only would that be operating outside their mutual missions, it might be misconstrued as cooperation, for which the barrier island seemed to have limited resources.

Her stomach growled as the screen door slammed behind her, directing her toward the kitchen. Renovated in white tile backsplash with gray countertops and floor covering, she had punched up the color palette by adding fuchsia everywhere she could. Opening the glass-fronted pantry, she grabbed a can of tuna and lamented her low cost lunch. Mindful to reward herself with an afternoon adventure, she slid the can under the opener's blade and pressed down.

"Maybe this would be a great day to get those photos of Saint Andrews By-the-Sea." The tuna can made its rounds. The smell of fish soon permeated the air as she considered her options. While on the island, she might as well take a dip in the ocean and recreate like everyone else.

Buoyed by the plan, she drained the tuna in the sink and dumped it into a bowl. Adding a dollop of mayo and a spoonful of relish, her choice didn't turn out half bad. Never mind that everyone else seemed to feast on shrimp and flounder. She'd be happy in her economic phase and enjoy the scenery while saving for something lasting. With everything loaded on her tray, she walked out of the front door and settled onto the slats of a wooden bench. A jet ski zoomed past, unzipping the water with its maniacal speed.

"What a waste of water space," she muttered, bowing to ask a blessing over the food.

~

Tyde leveraged the crowbar under the nameplate and pulled back with relative ease as the nails came out of the weathered wood. The demolition had to begin somewhere, and he decided to start it from the front porch and move around the cottage counterclockwise.

"Just like a hurricane," he joked, his words empty though his hands weighed full. These salvaged ship nameplates had the most history riding on them and he planned to protect them until the historical society could make up its feeble collective mind as to what their final disposition would be. In the interim, he would need a place to stack them and he searched the porch where viable options were few.

He finally decided to place them under the fish cleaning station which provided the only hint of shelter nearby. All else proved to be hammock stands, broken porch railings, and rotten floor joists. Maybe the time *had* come for demolition, but why did the end of an era have to fall under his watch? He surrendered the first freed nameplate and moved down the porch, helpless to remedy the deterioration behind the nails.

The sun glinted off the sound and held his fascination while his crowbar rested. How many of his relatives had stood where he was only to watch life pass one day at a time sound side? How many times had his grandmother called them in to dinner from this same spot? Those golden memories would last long after the weathered hull of the house disappeared. He would cherish those recollections forever. Maybe it was the fear of what came next that caused him the most trepidation, as he hadn't the faintest idea where he would live once the old homeplace fell, reduced to splinters and sawdust. The crowbar found the next candidate for preservation and he extracted his thoughts from the threat of the unknown.

~

With excellent late afternoon lighting and clouds playing along, Marin captured the old church in its aging glory. The sun at her back, she had taken shots from every angle she could imagine, even laying on her stomach and shooting through a bunch of red and yellow gaillardia blooms. The flowers seemed to lend the old gray edifice some color power and borrow serenity at the same time. Satisfaction buoyed her spirits. She stowed the camera and stepped back to the little parking lot. Traffic whirred by on the beach bypass. As dinner time approached, everyone seemed on the move.

She checked the time on her cell phone about the same instant the idea came to her. If she left now, she might be able to catch a certain crab harvester and make his rounds with him. The thought of it tickled and seemed like much more fun than bodysurfing on the churning edge of the ocean. Her pulse raced as she jumped into her car with the hope she wasn't too late.

~

He'd been so involved with his house undecorating project that he'd about let the sun slip away from him. Tyde grabbed the bucket from under the faucet and hit the step stones en route to the sound. An easy urgency settled on him, underscored by his familiarity with the routine and his languid approach to spending time on the water. He'd made it as far as the road when an unexpected visitor's car pulled into the cottage drive. He stopped dumbfounded in his tracks.

A woman emerged. "Is that invitation of yours still valid on a holiday?" Marin removed her sunglasses for accentuation.

A funny feeling closed his windpipe that had been sucking salt air just fine only moments before. Aware that his hesitation might seem like a negative response, he got his feet to cooperate and moved in her direction. "No small print written at the bottom for exclusions— only an open invitation." Trying not to look so stunned, he even tossed in a smile, though it felt odd like his cheeks were cracking. He slid his hand in hers and tugged her toward the road, allowing her only an instant to lock up and fall in step. "The sun is getting away from us again."

"So let it." She gave him a coy look before replacing her sunglasses.

Why that made his heart speed up, he wasn't ready to admit. Her blue gaze seemed to sparkle nearly as much as the sound waters at high noon and had a similar effect on him. "Get the anchor line, will you?" He turned from her to set the bucket in place. The water rippled around his ankles as she met him with the weight balanced in both hands. They brushed with the laden exchange and he stepped closer to help her in the boat. With a push, they were underway on a holiday cruise for two. When she took the bow without being asked, he settled into his power position feeling weak as a kitten. *What in the devil was happening?*

~

Marin propped back on the gunwale with her elbows. "Tell me some little-known islander lore." She seemed to examine the sun's direction and then pulled off her T-shirt to sunbathe. Her bathing suit wrapped her with the stunning colors of a coral reef.

His lungs seemed to go underwater, leaving him short of breath.

She leaned toward him with all her curves. "Tyde— are you okay?"

He slammed his eyelids shut when the sensation became much worse. "Just getting my sea legs, I guess. I've been up a ladder most of the day."

"Okay, let me do the talking then." She made herself comfy in the bow.

He took an oar stroke and nodded in relief. His gaze scampered across something he trusted, the horizon.

"I took some photos of the old Saint Andrews Church this afternoon. I'm working on a collage melding the history and natural history of the island for a big proposal at the end of June. It's an ambitious undertaking, but I think I'm on the right track."

"I should take you over to Nags Head Woods where the forest sets its roots for keeps." He aimed the bow toward the first float.

She dangled her fingers in the water."Haven't been there yet, but I accept the offer. I've got this coming Saturday free, if you want to go before crabbing time."

Now what had he done? She probably thought it would be a date or something. Well, what could a walk through the woods hurt—he being a local and all? "Meet me here at ten-thirty then, and we'll try to beat the heat of the day." He dropped the oars to free his hands.

When she turned the bucket up and slid to the stern, it struck him as fortuitous, like she was complementing him in the way of a boatman, without words cluttering up the place. "Good move." He hauled up the trap line. The pot appeared and he counted eight crabs that had dinner special written all over them.

She reached toward him and unfastened the trap door. "This is better than last time."

"Yes, better than last time," he echoed with an easy smile as he shook the crabs loose. Before he tossed the pot over, he dug a meat scrap out of a zippered cooler and refreshed his bait. She wired the trap closed and he tossed it back to the sound.

"What's that you're using for bait?"

He sat beside her and swished his hands clean before reaching for the oars. "Chicken necks, crabs absolutely love that stuff." He pulled a strong stroke further out into the embayment. When she giggled, their gazes met and he had to laugh with her, the sound was so infectious. "Don't worry—I won't bring any chicken necks to the woods on Saturday."

"No, let me pack a picnic lunch." She captured one of the oars from him. Using both hands, she rotated it in precise timing with him, centered enough to make forward progress.

Again, the pleasure of her company filled him as his gaze scanned the water's surface. They took another stroke in synchrony and he recalled a somewhat better offer coming his way and wanted to share it. "Only if you let me take you out tonight," he countered. "Jimbo has dinner for me on Mondays because business is light. He wants to keep me fat and happy."

"Don't forget it's a holiday Monday." Her brow

knit with the warning.

"That won't matter to Jimbo. Plus if he needs help, he's not afraid to ask."

"Guess I won't go bodysurfing later then, in case I have to resurrect waitressing skills from my barbeque joint days."

In a devilish prank, he leaned over the gunwale enough to rock the boat. She slid on the bench and clutched his waist to keep from falling overboard. "I'm happy to let you go swimming if you'd like to." He enjoyed how she'd wedged under his arm. With her coconut smell potent from this proximity, he could see her blue eyes sparkling under the rims of her glasses. Struck silent, he took in the scenery and let her fill his senses.

"I'm not swimming with all those crabs in this water." Resolute, her lips practically stroked the skin on his neck.

He felt her laugh before he heard it, replying with a quick hug before releasing her back to the unclaimed side of the stern.

"Paddle onward or Jimbo will sell out before we can get this fresh shipment of crabs to him," he replied in self-defense. Crabbing seemed less risky than the waters of mixed company, and a little more predictable. The next float came alongside and he hurried off the stern bench to get some cold-blooded crustacean flesh in his hands.

~

Marin had driven by the restaurant a hundred times, but had never given it much notice before. It looked like a no-frills affair, but the aromas wafting off the back screened porch spoke of sumptuous seafood laced with bay spice. Tyde led her up the rickety back steps and dragged the bucket along behind them. She opened the door and stepped into a full working kitchen. Though the parking lot sat half empty, the kitchen bustled at full steam. A blue-flecked pot boiled over as they entered and Tyde grabbed a pot holder and slid it from the burner.

"Steam pot's up," he said.

A heavy-set man appeared, wrapped in a white apron. "Aha—the crabs have arrived. Deliver this to table five—two couples in nice clothes." He nodded at Marin. She stepped to the stove without hesitation, donned the oven mitts, and hoisted the pot by its handles.

"I'll steam the crabs," Tyde said. He smiled as he hoisted the bucket.

She made her way through the swinging doors. After the table service and refilling two sodas, she returned to the stifling hot kitchen. The cook stood in front of a chopping block and he couldn't seem to make his hands working fast enough. Marin paused at the double sink to wash her hands.

"Out of coleslaw," the big man lamented as he reached for a knife.

She relieved him of the weapon and had the cabbage head cut in half before he could object. "Four years in a barbeque joint makes me the local expert on coleslaw."

He saluted and backed away, taking something sizzling off the grill beside her.

She soon pummeled the vegetable into submission and looked for the carrots to grate. Tyde swung a full poly bag in front of her and she snatched it with a lusty laugh. An apron flew over her head and someone cinched it from behind, tying it tight with efficiency.

The owner balanced two plates of seafood fresh off the grill like a salute. "Welcome to Jimbo's Seafood. We hope you'll come again."

Tyde held the door open as the chief cook and bottle washer made his way to the dining room. He brushed up behind her to start some fish fillets on the grill next. "He's great, isn't he?" His voice sounded husky.

She could have been happy doing any manual labor, as long as Tyde stood beside her. "Maybe a little understaffed—but great in an institutional kind of way." She pulled the refrigerator open to look for commercial grade dressing. Removing a jar from the door rack, she returned to her project and searched for an adequate bowl.

Jimbo sauntered back in, saw her predicament, and popped down a big enamel bowl from the shelf above her. "Add more carrots." He shuffled over to the grill.

"More carrots, barbeque lady," Tyde teased in a whisper behind her.

She pressed her lips together to deny him the reward he sought. Something tapped her backside and she glimpsed his antics with the flyswatter as he lunged at the screen door.

"String up some shrimp for the little lady," Jimbo ordered.

After a few more swats, Tyde retreated to the sink and soon began to skewer a handful of shelled shrimp. "We locals sit out back on the screened-in porch," Tyde said as he turned the fish fillets behind her. "I'll sneak you in on my passport since you made me the star of Sunday's paper."

Ironically they had walked into the delivery port for a drop off and had somehow gained a first class meal. "Sounds cozy." She turned with a wink to deliver the slaw to the refrigerator.

"Catch this last table with the grilled fish and you two can eat." Jimbo exited for the walk-in cold storage.

"He truly needs more help," she replied as she wiped the door handle with her apron. "I can spare a couple of nights a week, but only if you step up, too."

"Let's see what Jimbo says after we get a bite to eat," he replied. "I like to make my decisions on a full stomach."

She snickered and tried to poke him with a finger but he dodged her antics. The sound of sizzling cornmeal caught her attention and she pulled a batch of hushpuppies from the deep fryer a second before the timer went off. She clipped the basket to a wire ledge and let it dangle to drain the grease.

That instant, Tyde appeared with two empty plates awaiting the fillets. "And you thought your restaurant days were over," he teased, his eyes animated.

With strawberry blond hair curling out from under his perpetual baseball cap, Tyde possessed a sturdy handsomeness. She connected a few of his freckles together subconsciously before their gazes parted, startled by Jimbo's reentry.

"Go eat before you fly away like two twitterpated lovebirds." The cook snatched the plates from Tyde and headed for the dining room.

Marin squelched a laugh and turned to retrieve the coleslaw, setting it on the counter. Her apron untied itself and swung loose, prompting her to set it free. She claimed her dinner skewer beside a local yokel full of intrigue with silver-rimmed eyes like the sea. Yes, the fathomless sea.

Chapter 3

Tyde slowed the cadenced flip-flop of his stroll to allow Marin to take a photo of the entrance sign at Nags Head Woods. The tree canopy arched over the entrance road and made an effective backdrop for the marker. Not that he was looking at the trees, as her summery outfit stopped short of her knees and he could make out every flexing muscle in her tanned legs. Now he'd have something interesting to default to if the birds laid low because of the rising midmorning heat.

The forecast promised a high of ninety degrees, but the back of his neck registered more. He switched his hat around backwards since he'd remembered to sunscreen only his face. "Ask yourself why this maritime forest is here." The clues were there, if she knew how to read them.

Marin turned off the camera and pocketed it. She looked around as though the answer might be written somewhere. "I thought we drove past some old dune ridges on the way into the parking lot." Her visor popped off and she fanned her face with it as they stood in the wide open sun. "Let's head for tree cover until I get this figured out."

He stuck out an elbow and she laced her arm through his, the click-clack of his sandals reviving once again.

"Maybe the trees are more sheltered here. Aren't we near the backside of the island?"

"The backside serves as the safe side." He swept his hand to simulate the island's width. "The ocean side is where the overwash occurs, like in a storm when big splays of sand are shifted across the island's interior. Of course, the storm surge has to breach the primary dune line to accomplish that, but it happens more often than people realize."

She lured him toward the shade of a towering pine tree. "And what happens to everything in the way of that sand?"

"The vegetation gets wiped out down to ground zero. The growth clock starts back at square one and pioneer plants reinvade bare sand to lead the cycle."

A bird chirped nearby and she halted to listen. "It must be hard to grow a forest like that.""Right. Trees take time, so if you ever see a stand of trees on an island, you know that area stays fairly stable. That relict dune line you mentioned stands as its protection."

"So the sound side is less threatening—to plants and to people?"

"Oh, the sound has been known to carve a new inlet or two if pushed into surge by a hurricane, but you don't get the sand burial from the backside of the island, which is why every island is migrating toward the mainland. For me, that will be a sad day when those two connect, but fortunately it will take longer than my lifetime, so I'm good as an islander for the interim."

"How come you know so much about all these island dynamics when you seem to be just a crab collector by trade?" She pegged him with an inquisitive look above the rim of her glasses.

He pulled her down a sandy path and they disappeared into a dense wax myrtle thicket shoulder to shoulder. When they popped out on a small pond, he stared down a wading bird that had frozen mid-stride. "I'm an outdoor recreation graduate from East Carolina University." His gaze remained locked on the pond. "Go Pirates!" he added with mock pride. "Couldn't you tell by the way I rowed my boat?"

"Let's say I knew there was more to you than meets the eye, but I didn't get that from your rowing stroke," she replied. When her hand slipped across the bend of his elbow, the little blue heron across the pond lost its nerve and took wing.

Tyde's heart exploded with the wing beat—or had it been with her touch? Either way, the wax myrtle thicket wasn't letting in a solitary breath of air and he fought the urge to run. "Much too humid here. Let's bolt." He made good on the threat and pivoted back down the path.

She followed several steps behind. "I never like to double back on the same trail."

"Yes, ma'am, I'll keep that in mind. These side spurs require limited backtracking, but we can loop the rest. I want to maximize your entertainment pleasure, after all."

She fanned her face as she rejoined him on the chipped bark trail. "I might have seen a bush with tiny white flowers all over back there, but it looked like an oak. What was that?"

He looked around and finally spotted a familiar shrub in full flower. "That's yaupon, the local holly. By late fall, it will be covered with red berries."

"That would look great on the mantle of my cottage by the sound. I like bringing in the greens for Christmastime."

"The native Indians boiled these leaves as an emetic, certainly not my cup of tea." When her face squinted with a puzzled look, he grabbed his throat and faked retching so she'd get the full graphic picture.

Marin laughed and folded her arm across her stomach in response. "Guess I'll settle for the berries then," she quipped. "This is great having my own tour guide. It's a real treat."

"That'll be a dollar fifty, ma'am." He held out his hand.

She took it in hers and wouldn't let go, keeping pace with him down the trail. "Today I'm paying with a picnic lunch. I try not to pay with real money. It's overdone."

He chortled and allowed her to keep his hand captive while the sensation of being connected inched through him. She certainly made the day have an ease to it, no matter how much heat came his way. Now if only the breeze would pick up and let him breathe. "Find us a picnic spot then, as I'm about famished already." He swung the basket like unnecessary cargo.

"Now on the lookout," she replied. "Hey, you never let me know how you liked the preservation article I wrote for the Sunday Advance. Did I get everything right?"

His mind tumbled over the lyrical text,

remembering how she waxed poetic over someone else that seemed to be walking in his exact footsteps. "Well, the facts were dead on." He rubbed the back of his neck bothered by the heat again. "I don't know about the part where you likened me to the water strider. I guess they call that journalistic license, don't they?"

"I have to write from my perspective, as it's the most genuine angle I have." She stared at the trail ahead.

He looked at her to see if she flinched under the accountability pressure, but her countenance remained earnest above question.

"When I see you out there on the sound, it's like a scene from another place and time. Something like that seems hard to capture with words, as the English language falls short on occasion."

The heat moved straight up his neck to his cheeks under her unfiltered admiration. He wasn't used to the sensation. "I'm burning up in here. Let's try to break out of the forest and see if we can catch a breeze somewhere that has a touch of shade."

"It looks like the trail opens out up ahead. Sorry to drag you through the brush just to give me an education on maritime forests. Now I can really feel for the native islanders who had to eke out a living in the early days without air conditioning."

"Heat, bugs, and sand in their beds—not exactly a recipe for a thriving colony, let alone a resort community. No one lived on the ocean side in those days, anyway. Wanchese became the earliest permanent settlement—outside the lost colony at Roanoke, that is. It's a fishing village that time forgot along the sound side. They don't cater to tourists back there—or progress either."

She laughed at his last disclosure as the myrtle thicket opened to a decent high spot overlooking the sound.

A water-birthed breeze cooled his face and he set the picnic basket down beneath the crown of a midsized hickory tree.

She tossed open the basket's latch. "Give me a few seconds to get us set up."

Tyde took a deep breath and gazed over the sound, noting the channel markers as the gulls cried in the distance. He braced his hands on a lower branch and soon felt the tickle of a resident insect creeping across his knuckles. Clapping, he sent a shiny beetle on a journey to another exploration site.

Marin stood to offer him a moistened hand wipe. "Maybe we should ask grace instead of applaud," she teased, her eyes peeking over her shades.

He took the wipe and kept her hand captive in the exchange, making her smile broaden. "Lord of all creation, thank you for the stable places in our lives when all else seems like shifting sand. Bless the food and the company, as both seem straight from heaven right now. Amen." He opened his eyes to find her fully staring at him, her glasses gone and her gaze excavating.

"See, you are a sound strider," she said with a level tone, "from another place and another time. Just like the article proposed."

He swiped the cleaning cloth over his hands and gave his neck the once-over to alleviate a sudden spike of heat at her inspection. "Well, don't send me back right now, lady journalist, as that tuna smells pretty good from here." She attempted to step away, but he caught her and gave her a hug under the arbor of the tree limb. "That's for the article and your sympathetic perspective, even though I'm a soon-to-be refugee, not an aquatic insect."

She broke from his grasp in a playful reaction. "Well, you *are* attracted to my picnic."

He smirked to kill the smile he felt popping up and knelt onto a vinyl tablecloth she'd spread in the shade.

Two cockle shells appeared for bowls and she divided the tuna salad between them, placing one in front of him. A tube of round crackers followed and she tore them open to make the lunch fare available.

One giant scoop later, his stomach pain met its ready remedy. Now if only his inner equilibrium could be restored, as he felt off-balance with the growing attraction for his picnic companion. A bona fide breach of his perimeter security, he could hardly trust what might transpire next after the hug. Maybe he should focus on the food and squelch the flirting, for now anyway. The heat of midday poured from above and reflected back off the sand, pressing them into the here-and-now, secluded under the hickory's ambivalent arbor of shade.

~

Marin decided to jostle the row boat's captain out of his latitude of indifference with a sense that something sobering had come over him ever since lunch. Maybe he had second thoughts about the hug he'd extended, even though she enjoyed every second of his touch. When Tyde leaned out to haul in the first crab pot, she steadied the boat as usual, but also brought an oar up and let it trickle water over the flesh his raised shirttail had exposed.

"Okay—who's the funny guy?" He brought the crab harvest on board in one fell swoop.

The cage crashed down on the bucket rim. She giggled and reached over to unlatch the trap door. "A little water fairy must have done it. You're bound to get wet anyway, right?"

A smile finally tugged at his cheek and he lifted the cage to shake the captives out. One hefty specimen missed the bucket and smacked down on her foot, raising a threatening claw.

"Yikes..." She froze, afraid to move her foot to safety.

In quick reaction, he grabbed the escapee from the back, avoiding its pincers and other flailing appendages while lifting the crab back into containment. "Tell the water fairy she's safe now." He baited the cage with an amused look and closed it with authority. With a shrug of his shoulders, the wire mesh rectangle flew to its new location on the sound floor. When he slid beside her on the stern bench, she surveyed the catch seething in the bucket's bottom. He pulled the closest oar into position and she handed him the far one, kneeling in the center of the boat.

"Maybe we can impress Jimbo with today's catch."

Tyde shifted his feet forward, trapping her between his knees. "Jimbo's a tough script to decipher. I know he's grateful for the weekend help though, and I sure appreciate the extra cash. I'll be paying rent somewhere before the summer ends and it helps to have extra dough on hand."

She knew there had been some backlash from the historical society upon the initial plan of action. "Do you have a demolition date scheduled yet?"

"On or around July twentieth, as best the demo company can tell me. Depends on the job they're on right now. That will leave me fully disenfranchised, like a man without a country. Maybe if I could get past the hurt of it all, I could make some decent plans for what comes next." He pulled the oars through a long stroke. "Sorry you have to meet me on my downward spiral, so to speak. Life's a little iffy for…"

She caught sight of the next cork bobbing up ahead. "You mean for something as interruptive as romance, right?" She tossed a blob of slimy seaweed overboard. "You've been a little distant ever since the hug at lunch, so I wanted you to know we don't have to go in that direction if you're uncomfortable with it." She spoke the words, but could scarcely sense any truth in them.

A cork banged the bow and he shifted forward without a word, so the impasse hung between them unresolved, the silence agonizing.

She took the stern bench and leaned away to counter his extension off the opposite rail as his hands worked the line to produce the next trap. It appeared over the gunwale teeming with life and she met him over the bucket to unlatch the trap door. A cluster of bluish-green shells squirmed into the bucket and seemed to cut a chink in his armor.

His face softened as he baited the trap and set it for the next harvest. "The sound holds sway over time for me, like it's got its own rhythm." He slid the trap back overboard. It splashed and he nudged her over to fit beside her on the bench. "There's a war going on inside me between what feels right for the moment and what's unfair for the long run. Quite honestly, I'm wrestling through it." Tyde cast his gaze on the far horizon.

She bowed her head in empathy. "Maybe that's what faith in God is about." She plucked the right oar from his grasp and pulled a stroke matched to his. "We live in the moment as best we can and trust God with the future, no matter how uncertain the next horizon seems."

His shoulders drooped. "You're preaching to a man who lives in a hundred year old house that's falling down around him. My whole world is set to change before I can even get my dream plan underway. Rotten boards and rotten luck—the old place has to cave in on my shift."

She sensed the hurt in his words and didn't know how to bring him back from the shadow of such despair. Praying for understanding, she looked out at the horizon and wondered what he saw that she couldn't. "What would that dream plan look like, say if we lived in a world that moths and rust didn't corrupt?" She took another stroke to bring the next cork closer.

"Sound side recreation," he replied. "You know—a small dock with sunfish sailboats, paddleboards, rowboats, and sea kayaks. Nothing motorized that would junk up the sound with engine noise, only passive recreation. I'm talking something similar to the kite rentals at Jockey's Ridge, with equipment available for the paying recreationist. One day the sound side will come into vogue, and I hope to be up there leading the way."

"I can totally see you taking the helm of that movement." She gestured across the horizon. "All this water to enjoy, but I understand limited access has been problematic. The recreation department has centered on that issue and is forcing it forward as we plan the future use of your property. Your family has been overly generous to offer it, and the powers-that-be aren't going to let the opportunity go to waste."

"One man's opportunity becomes another man's death knoll," he replied with a sigh.

"Does it have to be one or the other?" She shifted toward him with her brow knit.

He locked gazes with her about the time the next cork banged the bow. "Guess your land use plan will carry the answer to that." He rose with a shrug to tend the pot.

Left alone on the stern to figure it out, elements of public use and historic preservation began to battle for prominence in Marin's mind. When the boat lurched with his lean, her counterweight action reported in late, off-kilter, and out of rhythm. The effect left a lot to be desired, so she slid opposite his position and the boat leveled out. *What a tricky thing to be on open water in such a tippy craft.* She scarcely knew her place out here.

Chapter 4

The deep fryer sizzled and brought the kitchen temperature up well past a hundred degrees, if Tyde could trust his biological thermometer. He plucked the sticky T-shirt off his shoulders and studied the last order Marin had left. She seemed to have vacated the restaurant for the moment and the patrons out front had grown loud in an obnoxious sort of way. He left the grill and pounded through the swinging doors only to discover her at the ice dispenser, balancing the restaurant's hefty owner as he dumped a bucket of replacement ice into the top.

"Hey—the tide's out!" a man at the rowdy table called.

"It's high tide, man—really high tide," a coconspirator added as Marin shot them a glaring look.

He held his arms out as if to embrace the group, which set off another round of jeers and unsavory comments. "Well, well. The Grayton boys are honoring us with their presence this evening. How's your seafood, gentlemen?"

"Like life these days, fried to a crisp and a little salty," Lonnie admitted.

Tyde noticed his neck sunburn registered a bit on the severe side, which wouldn't serve him well later in life. "Here's a tip fellas, try our grilled menu and use some SPF 50 or higher while you're outside. Both your gallbladder and your epidermis will thank me later." Laughter erupted around him and he waited for it to calm down to normal rowdy level.

"Where've you been, Tyde?" Brent asked. "We haven't seen you hanging around much lately."

He shrugged his shoulders in response. He didn't owe them an explanation. When he caught Marin's stare from the drink bar, she sloshed a tea pitcher over its rim. He certainly wasn't going to bring her into this wolf's den, by indirect reference or otherwise. "I've been doing my imitation of the first little piggy by letting my house cave in around me." When Lonnie pushed his empty tea glass to the table's edge, Tyde rescued in out of reflex.

"Yeah, dad told us about the condemnation on your folk's property," Lonnie replied. "Nothing lasts forever, man. Life is just a sandbar in the surf. Some days you're underwater and have to hold your breath."

The glass twisted out of his hand and he turned to see Marin armed with a tea pitcher and a smile. "Hey guys, this is a friend of mine who works for the Dare County Advocates organization over in Manteo. Marin Evans, please meet the Grayton brothers, Lonnie, Brent, and Half-pint." Her eyebrows arched at the last moniker.

The third brother breached the tabletop like a baby whale. "Kyle Grayton, ma'am, and I'll take some of that tea if you have enough."

Tyde felt the discomfort prickle his spine when Lonnie gained interest as Marin walked around the table to refill the big guy's glass. "Guess one of us should get back in the kitchen."

She gave him a questioning look that got even more complicated by a family of four arriving into the reception area.

He held a hand out for the pitcher and released her to the up-front duty while he stepped toward the back.

"Hey, man. Why don't you guys meet us at the Nags Head pier tomorrow night?" Lonnie's sun-leathered cheeks crinkled into a mischievous grin. "Let's have a fishing competition like we used to."

"Sounds fun," Marin replied over her shoulder. Her ponytail bounced with emphasis.

Something gritty swiped against Tyde's gut, but he couldn't figure out how to get out of the situation to save his soul. The pier at night used to hold a certain swagger for him, as he couldn't see the waves rolling in, but didn't seem to mind their crashing under the pilings.

"Order up." Jimbo waved a chubby arm over the half door to the kitchen.

Pressured for commitment, Tyde felt himself capitulating against his better judgment. "Okay. What time?" He turned away from them to hide his halfhearted attitude.

"Let's say seven," Lonnie replied, getting nods all around the table. "Maybe Bushwhack can come. He's been around some lately."

Tyde's stride stiffened at the mention of the troublemaker. Maybe he should let bygones be bygones. Bushwhack may have let the rehab sink in this time.

"Okay, fellas. Seven it is. I'll bring the bait fish."

"And definitely bring the blond." Lonnie chortled and slammed down the rest of his sweet tea. He made a disgusting slurp at the end which sent the table into uproar again.

Tyde's fist took it out on the swinging door as he sought refuge in the kitchen. He wondered what kind of ordeal he was getting them into. He'd better remember to warn Marin and do his best to shelter her away from the crude brigade or her opinion of the locals would take a dive. Not that they didn't deserve it, but he was a part of that legendary group. She probably couldn't dissociate the good from the bad, at least not yet. He sighed and lifted the shrimp skewers from the grill where they were getting overly suntanned. *Not good, not good at all.*

~

The lights on the pier looked like teardrops from here. Marin clicked the lock on her car in the parking lot. A flock of seagulls screeched overhead as an old man slung fish parts over the rail from the cleaning station at the base of the aged wooden structure. She straightened the sheer scarf tied through her belt loops and instantly second-guessed her choice, having dressed a little over the top for the venue. At least her T-shirt was on the plain side, if she could keep its jewel neckline on her shoulders. She scanned the lot but didn't see Tyde's rusted-out Jeep anywhere. If she put her stride in amble mode, maybe he'd pull up before she connected with the gang.

A green flag flew from a pole by the concession

stand and she knew that meant perfect conditions for beachgoers. If calm surf equated to good for fishing, she might catch her first saltwater fish tonight. That would make a vast improvement over her dinner fare back at the cottage, and maybe she could even freeze some fillets for later. Of course, she'd have to sweet talk Tyde into cleaning the victims, as fish scales and sharp knives made her squeamish.

Laughter peeled from the pier's lower ramp and she spied the locals they were meeting. The three Grayton brothers hauled their poles up the ramp where another man welcomed them with salutatory jeers. Dressed in a black T-shirt and jeans, the stranger seemed ill-placed to her, given the day's temperature had peaked at ninety-four. She slowed her pace and gazed at the ocean for a legitimate distraction. A line of brown pelicans flew by low over the breakers and she longed to share their serenity. Certainly she would level off to find hers, once Tyde got there.

Two older men left the pier lugging a red cooler between them. That looked like a positive sign that the fish had cooperated earlier. Her feet betrayed her by angling right for the ramp. She could only loll about so much without it being obvious, after all. Someone hailed out toward the parking area and the younger brother waved at her. She gestured back and feigned a smile. Now that she'd been spotted, the outcome became inevitable. She had to report solo for fishing duty. Where in the world was Tyde?

~

He jammed on the brakes which was the last thing he wanted to do. The beach road turned into a parade of incompetence, and it looked like all clown drivers had reported for duty. This happened every time he came near the ocean, which only reinforced his deeply-held hatred.

"Go ahead and turn in if you want to rot your gizzard on fudge," Tyde called to the carload up ahead. Finally, they peeled off to the right at a turtle's pace, being careful to avoid the sand off the pavement's edge. He shoved the accelerator to the floor and saw his first glimpse of the pier through a break in the dune line. Now fifteen minutes late, at least he had the baitfish. Uncooperative little minnows, he wouldn't mind dangling them in front of something larger, not one second.

A glimpse in the rearview mirror revealed that a grimace had overtaken his typically casual demeanor. What did he care that Lonnie and the boys would be waiting for his bait? They weren't exactly the punctual type. No, Marin had been added to the equation, and that addition made a difference. He bristled that he hadn't asked her to meet him earlier so they could ride over together. *Could this be territorial angst?* He blew out a laden breath and slowed for an out-of-state car trying to turn left for an ice cream treat.

"Long live the parade." He tried to release the grimace and brake at the same time. Someone at the café table out front tossed him a wave and he waggled his left hand back and forth. Traffic stood at a standstill. He planted his forehead on the steering wheel and tried to squeeze Marin out of his mind's eye, but couldn't.

~

"Hey there, Grayton brothers," she said in a mock-cheery voice.

Lonnie turned to take a look at her, and the guy in

black hooked a crooked grin. They exchanged something small which Lonnie quickly pocketed while the youngest brother grappled with the fishing poles. "Let's wait for Tyde up by the cleaning station," Lonnie replied with a nod up the pier.

The gear transport fell underway before she could pose an objection. She realized she would be outvoted anyway. Salt spray wafted up from the breakers below, and the thick air made her slow down even more. The middle brother walked shoulder to shoulder with Lonnie and soon passed something between them. A curl of smoke went up and she realized they had lit a cigarette. The younger Grayton pulled himself up the ramp with an armload of poles on one side and a cooler on the other. When he smiled at her, she felt a little better.

"I'm Bushwhack, an old school chum of Tyde's," the man in black said.

She took a glimpse at his curly unkempt hair and noticed a scar running the length of his cheek. To divert her eyes, she focused on Lonnie's back and when he turned around, the bulgy cigarette came in full view. A whiff of the smoke provided the telltale clue that something low and illegal was going on. Fear seized her breathing mechanism and she found the rail, forcing her gaze downward. Before she knew it, Lonnie had moved beside her, way too close for comfort.

"How 'bout we get loose before Tyde gets here," he suggested.

"No thanks – I don't..."

His hand pressed her arm and gently pinned her to the wood railing, insistent that she join in. When he held the joint up toward her lips, she turned and made eye contact with the hefty younger brother.

"Come on, Lonnie. Ease up." Kyle shifted the poles so one tip jabbed his brother's shoulder. "You're giving her a hassle on our first outing together."

Lonnie grinned and brought the flame-tip even closer.

Once he violated her personal space, Marin couldn't let him continue. "I said no." Her foot rammed his shin.

Lonnie doubled over in pain and came up red-faced, his jaw set.

"Hold it right there, gentlemen," a voice boomed down the ramp.

She flinched away from the tight huddle and saw a man in a police uniform. At the sight of him, her knees turned to jelly and she had to grab for the rail just to stay erect.

The policeman hitched his belt as he stepped toward them. "Are you okay, ma'am?"

Marin squelched the urge to throw up. She honestly didn't know how to answer.

~

Tyde wheeled the Jeep into the pier parking lot only to discover a police car beset with blue whirling lights at the base of the pier. Dread turned to something else inside him, something he didn't know how to name. Even with the sun lowering, he recognized the Grayton brothers standing in front of the patrol car. He pulled into a space, killed the ignition, and leapt through the door opening. He broke into a run and cut a diagonal toward the trouble.

Finally, he saw Marin up the ramp, the officer engaged in conversation with her. As he motioned toward his patrol vehicle, Tyde amped up his speed.

The last thing he had wanted to do was expose her to his peer group unescorted. Now she had a lawman escort, and he seemed bent on leading her right back into the encounter.

"Lord, help me," he mumbled between breaths as he dodged the front fender of the last parked car. He slowed to a walk as Marin arrived at the car, and then overheard the policeman demand an apology. As the man turned toward him, he caught the familiar lines of his face. A sigh of relief escaped his tight lungs.

Lonnie blurted out a poor excuse of an apology and the others hung their heads in shame.

Tyde slid a hand onto Marin's forearm. "Are you all right?" The wounded look in her eyes told him everything he needed to know. He leaned in to pull her closer. "Put your arms around me and fall apart," he whispered through her hair.

She followed his lead and the dam burst on her tear bank, with sobs and trembles that would make a movie star jealous.

He flashed a pleading look at the policeman. "Officer Tate, can I take Marin back to my car and try to get her to settle down?"

"Go right ahead, Tyde. Just don't take off until I talk to her one more time. Let me deal with these jarheads first."

"That's a deal." He tugged her to his side and walked away from the pier. They made the trip without a word between them. He picked her up and set her into the passenger side of the Jeep, then jogged around to the driver's side. Annoyed at the interference, he shoved the fishing poles out of the way and reached for her to reconnect.

Her eyes searched his face. "I was waiting for *you*."

Tyde wanted to respond, but the fillet knife twisting into his heart prevented him from voicing an answer.

~

The boat bobbed beneath her as the silver-faced moon rose higher over the sound to restore her spirits from the hurtful encounter. Tyde waded out several yards in front of the bow, and lowered the bait bucket to release the tiny fish inside. Microscopic bugs cloaked by the darkness launched an attack, so she pulled the scarf out from the belt loops and draped her head with it. Tyde still hadn't spoken a word, creating more tension than she could bear. He poured the captives back into their home waters with quicksilver fluidity. A glint of light flashed off their scales as he let them go, a remarkable scene. Now if only he would come to her and resolve this unrequited heartache.

~

Tyde cleaned his hands in the warm sound water, alternating the bait bucket in his grip. Maybe he should release Marin next, tell her not to bother because he wasn't worth the trouble. He turned to the boat and found her kneeling on the stern bench, her head haloed with a scarf that caught the moon's shimmer and sent it back up again. He needed to say it, step up and admit he was a loser-local like the rest of the gang, soon to be homeless on top of that. The water lapped his ankles and soothed his nerves as he moved close enough to touch the gunwale between them. His perception waned from being aware of every part of the sound side setting to nothing else but the beautiful woman in his boat.

Marin's eyes shone liquid in the moonscape, her

gaze locked on him. "I'm still waiting for *you*." Her voice echoed across the water like a wake through the rushes.

He set the bait bucket in the bow and his hand accidentally brushed the edge of her scarf on its return. Entranced, the silky sensation drew his other hand up and there he stood, shin deep in his aqueous homeland caressing strands of her hair. His mutinous hands dropped to her bare shoulders and she leaned toward him in a hushed tremble. His heart took the next move as he forgot the loser speech in a shifting current of touch and mutual attraction.

"Come on out," he replied in a husky voice. Before he knew it, she'd slipped into his arms, coconut scented and soft in his grip. Their lips soon aligned, the kiss floating weightless between them like the moonlight through her scarf, reflective in its quest and tender as the night.

Chapter 5

Preservation might have been an option thirty years ago, Mrs. Baum, but the floor joists are sagging beyond repair," Marin said. "For goodness sake, there are gaping holes in the porch floor. I saw the structural decay myself when I went for the interview. Let's step back from your total cottage preservation scenario and see what the other viable options might be."

The elderly woman shifted in her seat as though forced to get comfortable with her suggestion. "Well, the trademark ship nameplates are obvious," Cordelia Baum replied, contempt lacing her comment.

Marin jotted a note in her ledger to record the point of emphasis.

"And maybe we could salvage some of that handsome weathered wood planking," Hazel Aydlett added. "You know, to use it in a reconstruction of sorts. On signage perhaps."

Marin noted her comment and glanced at the photo of the old house she had taken the day of the interview.

She tapped the photo. "What about the outbuilding there? Do either of you know whether it shares historical significance or not?"

"I haven't a clue." Mrs. Baum feigned interest in the narrow shack with a quick peek. Her response came closely followed by a headshake from Mrs. Aydlett.

Marin caught the sound of the front office door opening, but remained focused on her immediate task before it escaped through her fingers. "We only want this garage thing preserved if it has historical interest. Otherwise, it's a late add-on and should be cleared away."

"Don't be too hasty with your wrecking ball," a man interjected.

Marin turned to find a cleaned up version of Tyde standing in the conference room doorway. A white T-shirt peeked through the open placard of a royal blue polo, and he sported a fresh haircut that looked almost preppy for a beachcomber. Her heartbeat skittered at the sight.

Mrs. Aydlett beckoned him over. "Mr. Fearing, how nice to see you again."

His gaze met Marin's as though to ask permission, so she nodded toward the table and he entered the room.

Hazel cupped her hands around the photo. "Now what's this about the old shack beside the cottage? I thought it might be something, but Cordelia seems ready to dismiss it from any consideration."

Tyde slipped into a chair at the far end of the table. "I doubt the two structures are the same age, as the pilings for the shack are different."

Marin gave him the slightest smile to encourage his

further input.

"See, maybe that's why I'm suspicious," Cordelia replied, her chin tipped up. "Tell us what you know about it, young man. Anything might be a clue at this point, though it begs for onsite inspection to be certain."

"Grandpa Walt called it the 'row house' when I was a kid," he recalled. "He used to store all his boating gear in there—oars, nets, and such. He even kept an old rowing scull cradled up in the rafters overhead so it wouldn't take up space."

"Or maybe it was up there to keep you from putting your sandy little hands all over it," Hazel teased, a knowing look in her eyes. "He didn't want it mommicked up, that's all."

Amused, Tyde laughed and propped an arm on the table beside the photo.

Grateful he'd dropped in, Marin scribbled a note about the scull and motioned for him to continue.

"At any rate, the shed never seemed to be the same vintage as the house to me, the wood slats are narrower and they've taken the weathering over time more splintered. Grandpa might have known its origin, but he never elaborated on that to me. Not that I can remember anyway. You're welcome to send someone over to check it out."

"The main house dates back to nineteen twenty." Cordelia maintained her business-like pursuit of the structure's preservation. "It's not likely the shed predates that, but we cannot rule it out, I suppose. Let me bring you a book that has renderings of the early frame structures along the Outer Banks, and we can compare it with what we know was already here."

"And if Tyde, I mean Mr. Fearing, is willing," Marin added, "I can take some close-up photos of the row house and bring them back for our meeting next week."

Hazel glanced between the two of them. "Yes, I think you should, dear."

Marin froze her expression to hide any personal interest in time alone with the client.

Tyde openly displayed his interest by waggling his brow, which likely wouldn't be missed by the hopelessly romantic octogenarian across the table. "An afternoon spent together might be just the thing to get this investigation underway."

"At Mr. Fearing's availability, of course," Marin insisted.

Tyde glanced at his watch. "Any afternoon before Thursday is open," he replied. "My mother plans to come down to enjoy the cottage one last time. It's been her post-Memorial weekend tradition."

"I so admire Anna Lisa's artwork," Cordelia said. "She seems to capture the Banks like no one else can. I'd love her to paint my formal gardens someday."

Marin's recognition rose as she put the two local legends together as mother and son.

"Thank you, Mrs. Baum," Tyde replied. "I'll make sure she knows you're a fan. I should bring her to Manteo one day while she's down and let her visit your gardens. Are your famous roses in bloom yet?"

Her pale cheeks flushed with color as she straightened in her chair."At least eight of the twelve varieties are in full bloom, so this coming week would be excellent timing."

Marin looked up from her organizer. "My schedule

is open tomorrow afternoon, if that works for you."

He hesitated and the elderly committee members leaned forward in anticipation. "Yes, tomorrow's good with me."

She squelched a smile and typed the site meeting onto her schedule with a start time but left the end of the appointment open-ended. There might be a rowboat ride at the end of her day, but one could never be too sure.

Tyde leaned back in his seat. "I'm already removing the ship nameplates for historic preservation, even as their backdrop hurtles to earth's surface like a meteorite." When the committee members giggled in response, he flashed a brilliant smile.

Marin made note of it in her heart. Something was falling all right, but she doubted it originated in the cosmos. Ending the meeting with the close of her ledger, Marin allowed the participants to linger another fifteen minutes, enjoying each other's company. Such rapport would serve her well in the long run, even though her stomach had been calling for food reinforcements with regularity.

Finally the elderly women stood to exit. Ever the gentleman, Tyde walked them out to the parking lot. With the door still open, she could hear the car doors close as she stashed the ledger in her desk drawer and tidied her desktop. Before she was aware of him, Tyde stood in front of her, hands on his hips.

"Well, you certainly know how to handle the ladies," she quipped, unable to hold the smile back. "And you most definitely look sharp today… which I'm guessing may have something to do with your mother's arrival this week."

"Exactly. She's weighed down by these expectations of my success in life, so I have to ante up now and then. Let me know if you like the new look—after I bribe you with lunch."

"I'm starving, so how can I say no to that offer?" She bent to retrieve her purse from the bottom drawer.

Tyde braced across the desktop and snagged her gaze.

She stood ensnared by his close attention. His trimmed hair now emphasized his silver-rimmed eyes and she became a willing prisoner, at least for the lunch hour.

He scanned her features. "Your directorship suits you."

The heat rushing up her neck begged for escape through the open door, so her feet stayed faithful and drove the detachment.

She'd made it halfway across the room before his hand apprehended her elbow. "How does a wrap sandwich down by the waterfront sound to you?"

"Perfect, perfect, and perfect." She slid past the threshold.

He held up two fingers but seemed to have a hard time accounting for the third.

She raised a solitary finger to indicate her added factor and wiggled it into his side.

He moved closer in response, swept her into his arms, and hoisted her into his Jeep.

Carried away from the mainland of life as she knew it, the effect proved as buoyant as a little row boat on the sound. Marin rode shotgun, a happy passenger.

~

The midafternoon heat rendered the colonial

reenactment site more authentic as the shade from the wax myrtle thicket opened up to the wharf where the double-masted square rigger awaited. A breeze blew off the water as Tyde peeled off his outer shirt and stuffed it in his back pocket. Sedentary actors snapped to life when they appeared, a contrivance that solicited a giggle from Marin as she stepped onto the entrance plank.

He'd determined that she needed a heavy dose of history after she failed to recognize the Elizabeth II from the Manteo waterfront at lunch. After she mentioned that one of her board members played a key volunteer role in the reenactment community, he had managed to talk her into the touristy excursion. Maybe life below deck would hold a certain charm, out of the direct sun and afloat on the sound.

A man wearing knickers and a puffy white shirt had begun his spiel on deck as they hurried up the ramp to catch the act. After a tour around the helm, Marin focused on a rope-making rig and the volunteer effortlessly ran through the methodology. She slid behind the end peg and plied her hand at the age-old art, completing the braid in a flourish of efficiency. The guide tied the end with twine, cut her souvenir off, and handed it to her.

When she turned and beamed with pride, Tyde somehow sensed her pleasure. The mate invited them below deck next, so he hastened to the open hatch to help her down the swaying jute ladder. An elderly man waited in the hold, trapped like a prisoner of time. His eyes sparkled at Marin, and Tyde guessed they'd found the board member.

The character shoved a triangular pegboard toward

them. "A game of chance anyone?"

Marin ducked behind his shoulder, so he slid onto the adjoining bench to take on the resident champion.

"The sea takes a lot out of a man, would you agree, my friend?" He made the first move and jumped one of Tyde's pegs which left the red team weak in numbers.

"Oh, I don't know." Tyde fingered his piece. "She brings a lot, too." Quiet reigned for a few moments as he made his move, and took down a white peg with it.

The old man nodded, circling his fingers over the board. "All a man can do is stand on the shore and wait to see what floats his way." The sage game player walked another peg up toward Tyde's red fleet and released it, poised for trouble.

Chin in hand, Tyde studied the board and considered the salty conversation. "Unless, of course, the man isn't afraid to wade out—or take to the oars with a good boat under him." Tyde selected the rear peg and hopped it three times around his men deep into the heartland of the white team. With the captive pieces cleared, his win became inevitable.

The old man threw up his hands in defeat, his eyes smiling at his adversary. "Taking to the oars is the right answer, young man. Good move. Now, Miss Evans, you see what I do with all my free time."

Marin nodded toward him with a smile. "Eli Etheridge, this is my friend Tyde Fearing."

"What—a Fearing from the sound side? No wonder you beat me, young man. Your heritage on the banks supersedes mine. Sorry about the condemnation notice on the family cottage. Sometimes, time is a worthy opponent already two moves ahead of the best intended."

"Thank you, sir. Did you happen to know any of my folks back in the day?"

"Your grandfather and I fished the inlet together every fall. One year he lost his old jalopy to a rising tide because the fish were coming in so steady, we lost track of time. We had to haul the cooler over the dunes on foot that evening, so we cleaned those bluefish right there on the beach, hacked 'em into steaks, and packed 'em in the icebox once we got back in. Never did see that car again. Guess it became the first artificial reef off the Banks."

Marin placed her hand on the old man's arm. "Stories like that need to be written down, Mr. Etheridge, so we don't lose the local heritage for the next generation."

Tyde's heart grew light thinking about the shared fables of the old timers, when life moved slower and the islands were disconnected for better preservation of heritage. Now fast food chains dotted the banks, and one-upmanship seemed the aim for endless rows of new beach house construction.

Their earlier meeting flashed to mind and the shed poked out like a splinter. "Mr. Etheridge, if you were familiar with the Fearing cottage in the old days, can you help Marin with her current focus of research? It's the little shed behind the big house, the one grandpa called the row house. It looks too weathered to be original to the house site, so we're wondering if it might have been brought over."

Marin slid against him on the bench and rested her chin on his shoulder. It launched a different kind of investigation, a tactile one.

"Golly, we did all kinds of projects back there in

that shed," he replied. His fingertips traced wispy overgrow eyebrows as the details worked their way to the forefront of his memory.

Tyde snuck a hand behind his back, and Marin readily accepted it.

"Oh, we made wine from Scuppernong grapes more than once, which your grandmother wasn't too fond of. And there was the fall your grandpa wanted to smoke fish fillets and leave them hanging on the rafters to dry. We almost burned the place down on that adventure. And the raccoons ate all our fillets, those rascals."

Marin giggled. "Was the old racing scull up in the rafters when you hung the fish?"

"Yup, it was up there all right. He claimed it was part of the original building and he never intended the two to part ways. I thought he was waxing a little nostalgic, but I've done softer things myself since then. It's funny what time will do to you."

"Yes it is," Tyde agreed. He felt a poke in his back and couldn't halt the resulting smile.

"How's the master plan coming for the project, Miss Evans?"

She tucked in the corner of her mouth and seemed to give her reply extra thought. "You know Cornelia still wants the entire structure preserved, so I'm working on scaling back the preservation from there. I meet with the Recreation Department on Friday to incorporate their wish list, and then I'll try to balance the two out somewhere in the middle."

The old man reset the game board with ease. "You're definitely the one for that job."

Tyde rose to leave. "That's what I told her."

Marin leaned toward the old sage and put a reaffirming hand on his shoulder.

His blue eyes peered up at them through the bushy brow and he seemed wise beyond his years. "Remember, Mr. Fearing, the sea takes a lot out of a man. Know where your oars are."

"Thank you, sir. Feel free to stop by the cottage any time the mood to reminisce strikes. The demolition is set for the third week in July, but you're welcome any time before then."

"I just might have to take you up on that offer." He rose and offered his hand.

Tyde extended his hand and shook with the seasoned fisherman. It had a weighty feeling to it, like the salty heritage of living at the water's edge.

Chapter 6

Marin stood in front of the row house tracing its linear architecture with her gaze. Tyde had propped the double doors open, and she examined the unusual bracing pattern on the inside panels. She jotted several notes on her pad, and tried to sketch an outline of the outer frame with rather elementary results.

He tripped down the porch steps with a flashlight, having explained that the shed lacked electricity. After a quick glance at her sketch, he seemed amused. "Now add a stick man at the door and label him 'Tyde.'"

"Sorry, people don't make it into my book—only landscape features and historic building details."

He raised an eyebrow in response and stepped up a concrete ramp to the opening. "Let's look for some history then."

She pocketed the notepad and joined him for the adventure. As they passed the threshold, she could smell the musty tang of the decay process on the cracked wood.

"Disregard the clutter if you can. I tried to move things away from the walls but most of it was too heavy." He kicked at something left behind.

"Come on—channel markers?" She pointed to giant spin top-shaped devices teetering against each other in the middle of the floor.

He shrugged his shoulders as a disclaimer. "Uh, those are Dad's from his buoy retrieval days. Some juvenile delinquents rip off road signs, but his weakness must have been buoys. Let's blame the water since we don't know all the facts. They could have floated to shore."

"And he salvaged them fair and square, right?"

"That's the story I'm sticking with. Hey, with over a hundred years of accumulation, you have to come into this with a blindfold on your judgment."

"I'll see if that works for me while I'm looking for clues." She turned and backed right into him. "At least the company is good, even if he comes from a pack of hoarders." When he leaned back to deliver a smirk, she caught the scent of something sporty like aftershave. "Don't distract me, I'm on assignment here."

"I'm all business, but it does seem a little cozy in here, right?"

She pulled the pad out, made a note on the roof rafters, and drew an arrow to indicate the location of the scull. A better idea surfaced and she grabbed the camera that dangled from a lanyard around her neck to snap a couple of photos.

"There's the 'row' portion of your grandfather's 'row house' nickname," she replied, intent to dodge his cozy comment. She pointed the pen tip toward the boat tucked up in the rafters.

Tyde walked beneath it in response. "One day we'll have to take it down, maybe when the building gets demolished."

"Or relocated. We should invite the historical society over for that, if it proves to be of any interest, that is."

"Aren't you afraid we'll find some bottles of that old Scuppernong wine grandpa made?"

"Any relic makes good history when you're in discovery mode, right? Now bring your light down this flank and let's walk back the entire length of this side wall."

"I'm your keeper of the light, Miss Explorer. Stay close so we can make our discoveries together."

She thought that might have been his best idea of the day, since rubbing shoulders added a romantic edge to the adventure. She worked her way around the buoy obstacle and waited for him to catch up. "Can you focus on these boarded up windows for a bit?"

The light soon traced out the original rectangular portal where mismatched salvaged wood now patched across the opening. "Recent work here. Looks like grandpa's slapdash style. He had lots of woodworking projects, but not a great deal of craftsmanship to finish them off."

"No, not pretty, but it worked. None of his nails pulled out. I don't see anything of importance, do you?" She felt him brush behind her and heard him make a whistling exhale that skittered across her neck. Undeniably, the air movement felt good, as they had stepped deeper into the structure where the circulation wasn't as cooling. "Let's move on, you go first." Immediately, she felt him pull a finger into her back belt loop and prompt her down the wall in step with him. A smile gave her away and must have encouraged his next shenanigan. The light began to quiver against the slatted wall, and his boyish whistle became more prominent. Like an elf, the beam jumped up to the rafters and quivered back down again to rejoin the search.

"Okay. Do I need to hold the light to get this done right?" A hint of demand rode the request.

"Uh, make a note of that. Keeper of the Light becomes uncooperative in back corner of shed." He tugged the notepad out of her hip pocket to continue his bent to fool around.

When she turned around to launch the face-off, she found him standing much closer than she'd estimated. The flashlight beam spotlighted the thief shining up from under his chin, which did something dramatic to his reddish-blond lashes. Her stomach flipped under the effect. She had to draw a deep breath, musky smell and all. "What exactly do you want?" She regretted her word choice in an instant.

A scandalous smile emerged in increments on the perpetrator's face as he surrendered the notepad to her.

Repossession didn't have the fulfillment she anticipated, as something more mixed between them in the shed.

"Record what it feels like to be in here," he said. "Write it down so you don't forget."

She blinked trying to forestall his next tactic, but he only nodded at the pad. With a tilt of her head, she obliged his request and gave their surroundings a terse review before touching her pen to the page. "You know, this would make for a strong follow-up article for the newspaper." She fanned her face to quell the rising heat. After a page of scribbled impressions, she turned the pad over and flashed the entry at him. "Are you happy now?" From his intense gaze she knew what his answer might be, which made her take a step back. Ancient wood studs soon poked her shoulder blades as she tracked the swirl of dust particles across the light beam.

His free hand swept past her and he braced his weight against the wall. "I wanted to tell you that I'm glad we met… before all this is gone, I mean."

She certainly hadn't expected that level of candor here in the dark, dank recesses of the shed. When she shifted her weight to her left foot, she must have given the appearance of moving away from him as he seemed incredulous. "It's been… unbelievable for me," she admitted, hoping to make some reparation. When the light beam shifted to her chin, she allowed him a few seconds of reconnaissance while she held her breath. She tucked the notepad back into its berth about the time he touched her hair. Her perspective of the shed now changed by the moment as it became part of the mariner standing in front of her, an elemental mix of heritage and hope.

His sun-bleached brow seemed to lower until their foreheads touched and the heat was no longer skin deep. In the next few seconds, her frame plunged into history as she closed the gap between them and paid homage to the man who held her light. The first kiss was only half as enjoyable as the second one. Unattended seconds ticked away into the realm of touch.

Tyde drifted away breathless. The lighting went

erratic as he wrapped her in a one arm to conclude their private embrace.

When she turned her head to regroup, a marking on the wall caught her attention and she froze. "Tyde…shine the light. There's something on the wall here." She stared into the corner. The light beam centered on the clue and the engraving came into full focus.

"Good glory," he replied in airy wonder. He leaned against her shoulder.

At the scant touch, her thoughts ricocheted in a thousand directions. "LSS No One," she deciphered as she traced the block print with her fingertips. "Does that mean anything to you?"

"Lifesaving Station Number One," he replied in a huff, like someone had punched him in the stomach.

She gasped in recognition and stared at the embossment like it couldn't be real. "No way. I don't believe this at all." She turned to face him.

His tanned face drained to deadpan. "Hoarding might be one thing, but this equates to trespass of higher magnitude," Tyde confessed in a whisper.

She pulled out the notepad, held a single sheet against the etching, and ran the pen over its surface to create a rubbing of the embossed image. Once completed, she stowed the pad and pulled at his arm.

He seemed afloat in a quagmire of related guilt. The nothing shed had turned into an ankle bracelet of heritage.

She stepped toward the entrance with him in tow. "Don't think of it as theft. Regard it as an act of preservation. You told me yourself, it's safer here on the sound side. If this is what I think it is, the Fearing family has preserved an authentic relic of Outer Banks history."

He stumbled into the direct light of day. "Preserved, not stolen?"

"Yes. For the collective good of the county," she added. "I've got Cordelia's book on early structures on the banks right here in my car. Let's see if anything matches up." Unable to contain her excitement, she jogged to the car. History begged to be unraveled right in front of her eyes. She found it exhilarating, especially with Tyde's enigmatic presence. Nearby, the waters of the sound lay unmoved, though her heart swayed like sea oats happy for the offshore breeze.

~

Tyde assessed the drawing and motioned for her to turn the page. "Not that one."

Marin hoisted the book off the porch rail and compared it to the structure that loomed to the west. "The building shape is right."

"But the fancy gothic trim isn't the same as our shed, is it? Maybe they got fancier as they moved down the coast, but I'd bet three channel buoys they didn't start out that way." He skimmed over the text trying to gain some insight, which proved difficult as she relocated the book to balance on the porch rail.

"Plain—and rectangular—with a double door up front." She flipped the page.

He stared at the next set of renderings and he thought his sternum would explode. A series of secondary outbuildings from the old lifesaving stations were depicted in sequence, a cook house, an oar house, and there, center page, was an exact tracing of his shed."A cart shed. Of course, it's a cart shed because the double doors opened to release the cart carrying the rescue boat for the surf crew.”

“Oh my stars. Your shed *is* the real thing, Tyde.” Marin slapped at his forearm.

A smile ricocheted into his cheeks and he looked up at the weathered building in a new light. Dizzy from the realization that a true island mystery stood in front of them, he grabbed the porch rail to steady himself.

“What does this mean? What does this mean?” Marin jumped up and down so enthusiastically, the floor joists began to protest.

“Better put a cease fire on your jumping unless you want to continue the exploration under the house.” He wrapped his arm around her waist to emulate a rescue. “You’re like a kid at Christmastime, you know that?” Her infectious giddiness reverberated up his arm. “If we have the ‘what’ part settled, let’s try to solve the ‘where and when’ aspects next.”

“Number One, Number One,” she chanted, making it singsong like a rhyme.

He flipped to the back flyleaf where an early nineteen hundreds line drawn map traced the Outer Banks, straggled out along the rim of the North Carolina coast. From the Virginia state line south, his fingertip passed over seven numbered stations with quirky names typed beside them. Several shipwrecks depicted off the shoreline made the lifesaving stations seem all the more necessary to safeguard the shipping route offshore.

“Station One looks like its north of Avon here.” He moved closer to the map. “Little Kinnakeet? I can’t tell if that’s what it says, the type font is so stylized. Wow, I never knew discovery could be such agony.”

"You're on the verge of a breakthrough—that's the agony. You should try to savor the moment instead of being so serious." She pressed her lips into a taunt.

Tyde collapsed the book and tucked it under his arm. "I'll savor the moment all right," he pledged, "all the way to Chicamacomico." His feet made quick work of the front porch steps as he headed toward the Jeep, and then thought better of it.

"Chico who?" she asked as she ran to catch him.

He hooked her by the belt loop and pulled her back into the shed doorway. "Take a picture with your minds-eye. Then file it and let's compare it to what we're about to see."

"Where?" She folded the shed door closed on her side. For good measure, she repositioned herself at the building's corner and snapped another photo.

He matched her with the other door and dropped the latch. "The most completely restored lifesaving station left on the island," he replied. He glanced at their vehicles and considered their options. "You drive, and I'll research the book some more. Okay?"

"Great. My car has air conditioning," she replied, fishing in her pocket for the keys.

Tyde tucked the weighty reference book under his arm, and considered adding a new chapter with the destination of their outing. Regret reared its ugly head that their discovery set poised on the annihilation of his home turf. He wouldn't let it poke a hole in his enthusiasm to get to the bottom of this mystery. No, there would be plenty of time for moping later. He eased into the passenger seat as Marin cranked the AC to high. Climate control seemed easier than history control, and he had none.

Chapter 7

Marin paused to take in the scenic beauty of the neatly arranged restoration. Surrounded by a white picket fence, quaint weathered wood structures sat in perfect array around what resembled a village square. Small gray outbuildings trimmed in white flanked the two-story station house like chicks around a mother hen. While Tyde stepped into the edge of a tour group outside the station house, she lingered on the periphery to view the scene through her camera lens. A unique perspective, it blocked out the irrelevant.

The tour guide's booming voice echoed historic facts across the property, so she surrendered her camera for the notepad, writing down the dates 1874 and 1911 as he went through his spiel. She scribbled down the timber frame construction called gothic gingerbread style, and reasoned that it explained the extra finials and arches on the station house that the other utilitarian outbuildings lacked. Maybe Tyde was right about plain dating back earlier. She would have to study the interpretive signs to verify that hunch as they looked for the matching building.

She stepped into the outer orbit of the core group as Tyde dropped out like a rogue asteroid. Their eyes met and she knew something was working on him inside. She wouldn't call it disbelief, but he seemed to be up against something major.

She wanted to offer him a rescue from the tour guide's banter. "I think we're better off on our own."

He nodded and pulled her away from the group as they rotated around the station house foundation.

"We already know what we're looking for, and that isn't it." She gave him a placid smile and pointed to the far edge of the fenced compound. "Let's go explore the outbuildings. They're plain vanilla with no extra sprinkles."

"Or those finial things," Tyde added. "I have a sneaky suspicion that, if our row house ever had those elements, Grandpa would have taken his hacksaw to them."

"I bet you're right. Doesn't seem like a Fearing trait to accessorize heavily."

"Except for nameplates, of course."

"Well, they make a statement, don't they?"

"Yeah, like 'read my history.' If the Banks could talk, they'd say the same thing."

They walked past a cluster of wax myrtle bushes. The maintenance crew had placed a circle of bleached-out whelk shells around them as an edging accent. Striking her as a down-home touch, Marin bonded with the effect at first glance. "I'd have that feature in my yard."

He winked at her as though he already knew and caught her hand in his. They approached the first outbuilding and it stood far too square, with windows and an offset pedestrian door.

By reading the interpretive sign, she soon learned that the structure was the cook house, which had been rebuilt early on due to negligent fire.

He stood staring through the open door. "Talk about modern conveniences."

She stepped up beside him and didn't see anything that seemed remotely modern. "Let's fry our fish somewhere else." When she spotted the next structure, it seemed more like a lean-to than a stand-alone structure.

"Add-on." Tyde waved his hand for them to pass on by it. They rounded the back corner of the picket fence and his step seemed to stagger as they approached a building on the far side of the village square. It looked more than familiar.

She locked her gaze on the wide double door centered on the outbuilding's front and slid the notepad out of her pocket to aid her comparison. They were identical structures.

Tyde froze in place, as though to give her an extra moment. When she looked back up at him, he'd drifted a thousand miles away.

She laced her elbow through his for moral support. "How about we go walk into your great-grandfather's yesterday?" She squeezed his bicep, a solid knot.

His steps toward the building seemed robotic, as though he now operated on autopilot.

About to have a meeting with destiny, she wasn't sure how he would weather it. Maybe some greater perspective would pad the interface. "I somehow think this was always meant to be. And God always intended you to be the one who figured it out."

He turned to her in silent acknowledgment, and then pulled away from her steady dockage for independent interplanetary flight.

Allowing him a couple of steps, she readied the camera and shot a series of photos as he approached the structure, walked up the ramp's incline, and touched the doorframe with veneration. Her eyes misted. She defaulted to autofocus to gain the last shot.

Tyde called to her after reading the sign. "It's called a cart shed." He gestured for her to join him up the ramp. "See the men here in the picture, pulling out a cart with a rope spool? They used the rope to secure the foundering vessel, if they could. Sometimes, they had to use it to secure their own life boats."

"So the *boat* wasn't in here?"

"No, I was wrong about that. At least at this post with the larger station house, the boat was stored on the first floor on a rail system, near the keeper at all times. He worked year-round, but his surf crew only served seasonally."

"So your grandfather's row house was a cart shed?" She let him brood on her question while she photographed the interpretive sign showing the men handling the cart with its line of salvation. "You know, I think part of our mystery falls into place here. My mind is racing ahead as to how we let the rest of the civilized world know."

He shook his head. "They'll either hang me or hail me, but we certainly have to come clean with it."

A perfect disclosure scenario popped into her head and she stepped closer with a nudge to his shoulder. "I have an idea, so hear me out." She paused while her stomach flipped. "Invite the historical society over. It has to be in the next couple of days so this discovery comes off as hot breaking news. We'll show them the markings, and give Cordelia and her book of sketches the credit for the identification as a cart shed from one of the seven original lifesaving stations."

Tyde worked his fingers across his brow. "But which one? We don't have that part figured out yet and, even then, it's only a guess. Little Kinnakeet was Station Number One on the flyleaf map. We need a better map, one with more detail."

"I glimpsed a gift shop tucked into the station house building," she replied. "Maybe we'll find a reproduction map in there. We could make it available at the press conference with the historical society, and allow their brain trust to work out the location. Again, that gives them the spotlight and builds support. No one will throw stones at the Fearing family if we give the historical society a piece of the infamy."

He dug his toe into the concrete of the ramp, trying to dislodge a small shell that had been captured in a matrix of authenticity. "Mom's coming in Thursday morning. I'd like her to witness this hullabaloo, and be as big a part of it as she wants." His eyes searched her face for a workable answer.

"I have the recreation department meeting Friday morning, and you two were going over to tour Cordelia's rose garden. What about Thursday afternoon at one o'clock? That would give the representatives the rest of the afternoon if they wanted to follow up on the original location of the cart shed. I could take pictures at the press release, and put it all together for the local section of the Sunday paper."

"Yeah, I like that. We'd put it out there like an open-ended mystery. Be sure to put in lots of quotes from the historic society's board members. They're the experts and each one will have an opinion. That being said, please print only the *positive* ones."

"Don't worry, Tyde. I'm not going to sink my sound strider just because he has a valuable little turn-of-the-century shed in his yard and doesn't know how it got there."

"That's a mysterious shed harboring a phantom boat in the eaves."

She gave him an eye roll of appeasement and stepped off the ramp to take some photos from the side. With the same wood, the same weathering, and the same dusky smell, the two buildings had to be of similar vintage. She was sure of it. Time now of the essence, she took the pictures and quickstepped back to the ramp area. "Hey. Want to hang out here while I check the shop for a better map?" she asked, trying to hurry and be patient all at the same time. "I don't mind splitting up."

Tyde seemed mesmerized, leaning over the rail that restricted access as far as he could manage. "That'd be great. I feel like a need a few minutes to sort this out in my head."

"Great. I'd planned on getting a few more photos of the main station house once the tour group vacated. I see them in front of the cook house right now, so I'll scoot by and have the big house to myself."

"Get as many maps as you think is reasonable so we can spread them around the crowd."

"Good idea. Anything else?" Her heart raced with the thrill of their discovery. She had to make her mind focus as her imagination ran away.

His gaze warmed for a few seconds. "You're great at this, you know."

She decided to flip the compliment. "No, the Fearings are the true preservationists. You've salvaged the past for the rest of us."

He tried to shake it off. "Well then, I appreciate your levelheadedness. Left up to me, I'd probably hightail it and run."

"Okay, I'm making you a more stable person. Thank you—I think." She hooked a smile and left him at the carbon copy of his row house, allowing him the bonding time he'd requested. She might as well default to shopping to give him space to work through the situation, even if her spree only involved buying maps. A headline came to her and she extracted the notepad to jot it down. Two pages later, she arrived at the station house door, the gothic gingerbread cornice directly overhead. "Skip the fancy," she repeated as she entered the ancient structure.

~

Something seemed so right about this it made Tyde's head swim. The whole scenario unfolded like an extended déjà vu where you unravel some secret about yourself you never quite understood. The cart shed clicked into logical place. He never doubted for a moment he had to be the one to take the mystery public. He hated press conferences with a passion, but maybe this once he'd have to rise to the occasion—for the Fearing clan. Hang the drama, though. He'd put the discovery out there and let the historical society run with it.

A twenty-five by forty foot shed could readily be

dealt with, but what about a package of five-foot-two and eyes of blue? He swiped his hand over his chin and let the beard stubble poke some reality into his conscience. Marin sure had him off-kilter and listing to port on the inside. Every time they were together that unevenness overtook him, and left a wave rippling through his no-wake zone. He had neither seen her coming nor put a bulkhead in place to stave off the breaking wave of emotion she generated just by being close by. Not the type of mystery readily solved, he could at least man-up and embrace the telltale clues.

Movement by the tour group broke into his thoughts as they progressed toward him. With lanky regret, he withdrew from his place on the cart shed railing and backtracked. The thought occurred to him that maybe he should share his feelings with Marin while they still lapped at the high tide mark.

A mockingbird sang from the myrtle thicket, its call running liquid through the better portion of its thirty-two part repertoire. In lyrical trance, he stared at the thicket when the whelk shells somehow caught his attention. He remembered Marin had liked that touch, a bit of homey border on an otherwise wild world, similar to her effect on him. Hadn't he lived as boundless as the sound waters until her arrival? The circle shape didn't speak to him, but he knew a variation that might speak to her. With a quick glance at the departing tour group, he made sure the coast was clear before he bent down and began the rearrangement. The whelk shells soon spoke volumes for abandoned lumps of calcium.

Tyde brushed the sand from his hands and stepped out from behind the last bush. A lens clicked and he looked up to find Marin capturing the moment digitally.

He smiled because she had no clue what he was up to, and he stood more than ready to signal his intent.

She adjusted the camera's lanyard crossing her chest. "Want to tell me what you're doing back there off the trail?" Her eyes twinkled in the declining afternoon sun.

From the bag on her wrist, he could see rolled-up maps peeking out. "Well, we're at a lifesaving station, right?" He stepped onto the mown trail beside her.

She tilted her head, glanced at him first, and then studied the myrtle thicket. When nothing seemed to reveal itself, she gave him a more piercing look. "It must mean that one of us needed a rescue." She glanced at her camera and checked her back pocket for the notepad. "Sorry, I'm not getting this riddle, Tyde. Maybe you could spell it out for me."

"Or maybe you could read the message in these whelk shells and figure out the mystery for yourself." He made a sweeping gesture toward the thicket.

"Fine. I'll do just that." She handed him the bag and followed the right side of the circled border. She passed the first bush and stopped where the circle dipped into a v-shape. "A heart pattern? You rearranged this for me?" Her expression melted into tender regard. "Even if it is defacement of a historical site, I love it, truly love it. Why, it's the sweetest thing anyone's ever done for me. You knew I admired those whelk shells. They make me feel like a villager."

"Let me tell you how I feel." He inched close enough to lace his arm around her waist. "You make me feel like I'm floating even when I'm not on the water, like a breeze is blowing through me even when it's calm as daybreak. I'm falling off the edge of the horizon over you, Marin. I asked these shells to help represent by symbol what I hadn't spoken out loud."

"And you're telling me right now?"

"I'm falling for you, casting my hull against an unmarked buoy, setting sail on uncharted waters." He swirled the map bag around his head for emphasis.

She laughed and reached for him in a full-spirited hug. "What a day full of clues." She stayed tucked into his neck a few lingering seconds.

"Can you tell me if I'm on the right track?" His whispered tone held more beg than he'd intended. Despite the indiscernible gasp that escaped her lips, he didn't misread the smoldering response in her ocean-blue eyes.

"Tyde, you absolutely captivate me," she replied softly.

He pulled her tighter against him to celebrate the signal received and decided to give the touring group something to ogle at from across the square. Maybe they would recognize history in the making since the station they walked around claimed to be authentic. The candle wax smell from the myrtles wrapped around them and the mockingbird started into its playlist again while he kissed the object of his growing affection. The ancient village seemed to embrace the two of them by providing a charming backdrop for measureless time. That river of constancy managed to stand still on rare occasion, like the one that now held them together.

Chapter 8

Marin baked under the midday heat, but let her sense of purpose be her shade.

Cordelia Baum struggled out of the direct sun and took a step. "This had better be good."

Marin held her elbow as Hazel Aydlett trailed her far side. "Let me assure you, Cordelia. You won't want to miss a moment of this revelation. Tyde has some major news for us all, and I think you'll be delighted for coming over." She nodded at several men standing in the sand below, partly shaded from the industrious June sun by the stair rail. She caught the gaze of Eli Etheridge, knowing her board members attended as a show of support and could be called on without advance notice.

A well-dressed woman stepped out of the Fearing cottage. "Lovely Miss Cordelia, I knew you'd come. I even counted on it."

Marin saw the sour demeanor shed from the elderly woman's exterior as the lithe flatterer approached them. Relieved, she passed the woman's elbow to her new hostess and dropped back to greet Tyde.

He gestured to the woman. "Anna Lisa Golden, this is Marin Evans from the Dare County Advocates." He rested a hand on her shoulder. "Marin, this is my mom, here for her last week at the Fearing cottage."

His mother graced the elderly matron with a delicate shoulder squeeze and turned toward her for cursory inspection. "Hello, Marin. I've heard a lot about you, all of it glowing." She gave a tiny smile with the admission. "It's nice to meet you at last."

Overcoming momentary bewilderment, Marin managed to form a reply. "I guess I didn't put the two of you together, since your last names don't match. I've admired your artwork for years and hope to own one someday."

"Thank you for the compliment—and for taking an interest in Tyde. He knows I don't approve of his lone wolf existence out here on the sound. I paint under my maiden name because it seems more artsy."

When Tyde moaned, she switched her focus. To her amusement, he rolled his eyes as she dropped down the stairs to greet the next elderly member of the historical society. "We'll start in five," she said over her shoulder.

He stuck a finger inside the collar of his emerald green shirt and pulled it looser for resuscitation.

Next, Marin spied several overdressed members of the OBX Chamber of Commerce step out of a white SUV and take a few mincing steps onto the sand yard, a real feat for the woman dressed in a pencil skirt and high heels. "This will certainly be a day they remember," she muttered to no one in particular.

"Yes it will," Eli replied as he came up behind her. "You have us on the edge of our proverbial seats, Ms.

Evans. Something tells me your revelation will more than deliver the goods to this bunch today."

She leaned back to keep the exchange confidential. "Strong hunch, Eli. I've given the announcement honors to Tyde because his family has to take responsibility, good or bad."

His graying brow knit as he contemplated the options. "I'll try to steer the outcome toward good, if necessary, for the benefit of the current generation. No need to punish them for past transgressions."

"I knew you would understand. Now excuse me while I greet these chamber reps and get everybody in place." Marin left her guaranteed ally for the vagaries of more casual onlookers. When her gaze traveled past the chamber staff, she saw the Grayton brothers headed up the walk behind them. She'd have to bolster her mock gregarious greetings now, as her chest tightened under the threat of reunion.

"Good of you to come out today," she said to the chamber group. The tight-skirted woman took her hand and offered what felt like fresh flounder for a handshake. At least her smile was genuine.

"We're minutes away from starting, so if you'll take a place up by the porch we'll get right to it." Before she turned to greet Lonnie and the gang, a blur of emerald green passed her as Tyde headed off the uncomfortable encounter. She pivoted away from the rescue and headed back to walk through the growing crowd down below the porch railing. Hazel Aydlett tossed her a wave from up above. She returned the greeting and blew out a breath weighed with anticipation. Speculation would soon abound and she hoped to be adequately braced for it.

Anna Lisa dropped to the bottom step and motioned her over. "I've pulled a picture of Grandpa Walt for Tyde to show around."

Marin leaned close enough to smell a fragrance as light as linen. "Good thinking. We have to humanize this at every angle. More chances for forgiveness that way."

"I agree. Say a prayer for Tyde, as he's had lots of trepidation over this all morning."

She nodded and pulled away, sensing a bond of mutual concern between them. Tyde had the hands of a crab harvester, not a thief. Out of nowhere, the beatitude assuring blessings for the peacemakers came to mind as she strolled over to the crowd. She would have to claim that promise today, as being a child of God outranked being an arbitrator of justice over some historic misappropriation. Taking a handful of the rolled maps, she launched into the pool of spectators to rectify the breach of time.

~

From the porch railing, Tyde saw Darien Grayton chatting with his sons. His mother moved alongside him and he caught the impish smile the man greeted her with. A curve ball out of left field, he struggled to keep his concentration on the issue at hand. Second up on the speaker's podium, his leadoff spokesperson now headed up the stairs. With a disconcerted glance across his mother's face, he turned and pulled Marin toward him as she made the landing.

"It's getting hot up here for the elderly ladies," he said under his breath. "Ready to start?" She looked cool and confident in the flurry of setup, so he tried to siphon off some of her reliance by touching her arm.

"I'm ready if you are. Start the proverbial drum roll."

He transferred his hand from her arm to the sailboat emblem on his shirt. "That would be my heart beating out of my chest. It's now or never though. Let's do it. Straight up with no hype, just the truth as we know it and the circumstance we've been left to deal with."

"A-okay, partner. Wait on my cue and then jump into the fray with me."

When a steady smile dawned, it iced his nerves on the spot.

Marin took Cordelia's book from under her arm and slapped the railing with it. A shotgun would have sounded less deafening. The crowd murmur diminished and a laughing gull cawed overhead. "Good afternoon everyone," Marin began. A non-cohesive response echoed back and she nodded in several directions.

As if on cue, Tyde's focus drained away and a daydream of time-chiseled proportions overtook him. His grandfather idled in the yard below, hanging fish on the rafters of the shed as if he hadn't a care in the world. The row house looked the same, weathered and dated, even though the man in the vision seemed spry. He worked with rhythmic precision as he tied and hung the fillets, his captain's hat nodding with the routine motion. After the last fillet had been secured, he turned and looked up at the porch in satisfaction—right into his grandson's eyes. A gull cry pierced the sky overhead and the vision evaporated.

Marin gestured to the west flank of the house. "Consider the Fearing cottage an easel where dozens of priceless works of art have hung for decades. Thankfully, the Fearing family has already begun the meticulous work of removing these timeless nameplates salvaged from shipwrecks over the past century and will actively procure suitable housing for their future display. I think we can safely say that the Dare County Historical Society is positioned to make a recommendation for an honorable place of repose for these relics of our history from the Graveyard of the Atlantic. I personally look forward to that relocation and would like to thank the Fearings for their willingness to loan these to an admiring public."

Tyde fought to regain his focus as a spattering of applause rippled from down below. Right now, he couldn't even call his first word to mind. That might prove troublesome in the immediate future, as he was scheduled to speak next. His mother stepped against the rail and waved her appreciation to the crowd below, using every ounce of charm she possessed. At this point there was only one thing he could do. He pinched his eyes closed with his right thumb and index finger, launched a silent prayer up for proper perspective, and searched for a rational place to alight. When his body began to sway, he crammed the back of his calves up against the splintered wood of an ancient deck chair.

Unflappable, Marin continued her intro. "Knowing that the house—our easel for so long—has been condemned and is slated for demolition the middle of July, we now shift our focus to what of worth can be salvaged from this homestead. Anna Lisa Golden has generously donated the Fearing book collection to Dare County Public Library for inclusion in its Coastal Volumes collection. What is not catalogued there will be added to the book sale offerings this fall as a fundraiser."

Tyde squirmed at the news. A fleeting image of his father raced through his mind next, as the library had been his dad's favorite room. How many nights had he reclined on the threadbare sofa under the illumination of a solitary lamp, reading tales of the sea in some ancient adventure book? Where was Wade now? And what would he think of the dissolution staring them in the face? A sense of unfairness overwhelmed him, that his father should have some of this dubious responsibility, not Tyde alone.

He swallowed his disdain and tracked a distant cloud reflected off the southern horizon, as if the sound waters reached for him in billowy solace. This boat he would row solitary. God would have to help him navigate because he felt as lost as a shipwreck victim, trapped on the shoals and breaking apart with every wave. He felt a nudge and his mother glanced at him quizzically.

"Apart from the nameplates and the vintage book collection, our search for additional historic worth has taken a large-scale turn for the most interesting, which is why we have called you here today. Let me say that the search and its early discoveries have become indelibly etched into my heart and mind, so I hope it will strike each of you in a similar way."

Marin paused and rubbed her palms together. "Before I hand the podium over to our host family's representative, Tyde Fearing, I have a favor to ask. As we contemplate the possibilities of what is about to transpire, allow your reaction for today to be linked with both yesterday's hardship and tomorrow's hope for a life we cherish, a life full of quality not qualms. A life that builds for the betterment, not one that tears down the cooperative edifice of what might have been. Now, with the announcement of what could be Dare County's most prestigious historical find this century, I give you Tyde Fearing."

Mouth dry and knees trembling, he approached the rail as Marin's board members led a round of applause in response to her challenge. The recipe for disaster now written all over the horizon, his mind zipped across the surface of the moment like a black skimmer across the water. Marin turned and looked at him, confident and eyes afire with enthusiasm. Her gaze penetrated his confusion. A peace came over his spirit like a divine presence had attended him. In gratitude, he reflexively gave her an innocent shoulder hug which prolonged the applause and left him in a positive frame of mind. He released her and grabbed the rail, ready to face his obligation.

"Typically when we have this many people over, we're picking crabmeat over yonder at the fish station by the kitchen porch," he joked. A smile eased into his cheeks. A few hearty laughs rose and he heard the elderly contention behind him agree with an 'amen' or two.

"Honestly folks, I can't stand here today making this announcement without thinking of my grandfather knocking around in the row house there or my dad pouring over those treasured books in his library. I guess that's how it is with family as the years run together to build memories and a heritage. Scripture says God himself picks the land where we live, and we get to hold it as a proud possession. It's been every bit of that for me, and I still count it my best day when I can row out on the sound and come back home with a bucket full of crabs." His voice grew husky through the last bit of confession and he paused to swallow and set for launch.

"Let me turn our attention away from the main house and get to this discovery Marin has mentioned. Sometimes it's in the secondary culls that the gold nugget is found, which is how I can summarize what we've tripped on right here in the side yard. Grandpa Walt was always partial to the little garage out to your left along the northern portion of our property. Knowing that, I wanted to be sure we combed through the outbuilding, checking it for anything that might earmark the structure as unusual."

"Well ladies and gentlemen, we found out something about the shed we believe could predate the Fearing house, even before the turn of the century. But instead of telling you what this significant find might be, I wanted to show you and let you examine it so you can authenticate it for yourselves. We'd like to have everyone tour Grandpa Walt's row house in a loop, then return to these front steps and join us in an open session to discuss what we might have and what to do with it. Anyone interested?"

"I'm already halfway down the stairs," Cordelia replied, making quick work of the trip on his mother's elbow. Marin had Hazel in tow and the powerhouse foursome made its way down to the hoots and catcalls of the intrigued audience below.

"You've set the hook real fine," Eli Etheridge called back to him. "Come on down and reel us in. My old heart can hardly stand the suspense."

Tyde shot a ready hand into the air. "I'd be honored to lead the way. Let me get the power on for the auxiliary lighting and I'll meet you by the kitchen steps." As he crossed the wraparound porch, Tyde felt the wind blow like a cleansing stream and sensed he had the favor of the crowd on his endeavor, which must have been the grace of God. "Thank you Lord," he muttered under his breath as the crowd members plodded through loose sand to make their way to the outbuilding.

By the time he plugged in the extension cord, something of a line had formed waiting to start the loop of discovery. Down the stairs two at a time, he hoped the three block letters and their sidekick number would be more than enough relic power to steal the show. Otherwise, his reputation would soon be up there hanging from the rafters like a smoked fillet, cut and strung up by a history of questionable salvage, legal or otherwise.

Chapter 9

Marin gave a quick signal to Eli Etheridge as he towered above the two women studying the open book. He nodded and moved opposite them so they stood face-to-face. She stepped toward Tyde and gave him a confidence-infused look as the crowd murmured around them. Anna Lisa slid by his other side, cradling the photo of Grandpa Fearing in her elbow.

"Your verdict, Cordelia?" Eli's voice boomed to demand the crowd's attention.

The elderly woman glanced up from the page with firm resolve set into the familiar pattern of wrinkles residing on her face.

With the future direction of this inquiry riding on the historical society's response, Marin held her breath and waited for the verdict to cascade from this fount of local knowledge. Hazel and Cordelia shared an inaudible exchange.

The reigning president of Dare County Historical Society turned to address the crowd below. "As my Vice

President Hazel Aydlett and I agree, we are proud to announce that we are looking at an authentic outbuilding from one of the original lifesaving stations that protected the banks along Cape Hatteras."

Eli led the applause and gestured to the two women which deepened the accolade.

It landed on Marin's ears like music, as she had been afraid for the slightest of seconds that the outcome might not be in the realm of celebratory.

Cordelia held her hand up for silence. "We concur that it most closely resembles the structure labeled a cart shed, which became an addition to several stations in the refurbishment of 1892." The crowd responded with gasps at the antiquity of the shed.

Marin assessed the collective astonishment to translate it into her pending article.

"Which station it originally hailed from now becomes our operable question," Eli said. His inquisitive tone would help lead the conversation in a helpful direction.

"Well, it's clearly marked 'Number One,'" Darien Grayton replied from the crowd. "Find which station bore that moniker and we'll have our answer."

Marin unfurled her map with enthusiasm. "Time to use your maps, everyone." Informal study groups began to collect as the parchment maps garnered attention. A giggle erupted from the chamber reps as Lonnie stepped into their group to offer some local knowledge. Maybe research seemed a little outside of their wheelhouse, but becoming part of history might be deemed worth their effort. She caught Anna Lisa giving Tyde a crook of an eyebrow as the outcome hung over the compass rose of a reproduction map dated 1918.

"By all rights and order," Cordelia said, "possession must fall to Little Kinnakeet, Station Number One. That places us north of Avon in the first installment by James Boyle, with the original station dating to eighteen hundred and seventy-four."

Eli let out a low whistle that accompanied the crinkling of parchment maps across the afternoon heat.

"Only Hatteras Lighthouse would be older by way of comparison," Hazel added.

Marin held her peace and let the Historic Society process through the timeline that would validate their claim with authenticity.

Tyde wet his bottom lip, his gaze darting from speaker to speaker as his mother's delicate hand appeared on his tanned forearm.

"Actually, Bodie Island and Ocracoke lighthouses predate Little Kinnakeet as well," Cordelia corrected. "But this shed matches the dates on the restoration at Chicamacomico and the slatted façade certainly appears identical. You all know that Little Kinnakeet remains on our wish list for restoration in the society's master plan. If this shed turns out to be an authentic relic from Kinnakeet, that only fuels my passion all the more to get that overdue restoration underway."

"I agree with Cordelia," Hazel said. "We'll have to help the Coast Guard underwrite the costs to get that kind of preservation underway, what with the federal government in the quagmire of deficit that they're under right now."

"Well, I think this shed belongs to the public, not the Fearing family," Darien Grayton insisted, his tone accusatory and possessive.

A muscle in Tyde's cheek flinched as Marin took a

step up to lend her some height above the crowd. "Some of you might not be aware, but the Fearing family is currently in the process of bequeathing this parcel of land to the people of Dare County." She spread her arms wide to encompass the immediate surroundings.

Below, Lonnie pulled his outspoken father back into the obscurity of the crowd.

Marin fused her palms together. "Following the house's demolition set for next month, the land will be developed into a multipurpose public park which melds historic preservation and passive recreation here on the sound side. The Dare County Advocates organization has been tasked with developing the land use plan to accomplish that blend of purpose. I assure you, we'll do everything in our power to make it user-friendly for the people of this great county."

Eli began another round of applause, which gave her time to beckon Tyde up the stairs beside her.

"Before we let our boat get too far out the inlet," Tyde said, "I wanted to remind everyone that we have a second historic artifact awaiting our discovery, the part that gave Grandpa's shed the nickname 'row house.' You all saw for yourselves the rowing scull up in the building's rafters. The Fearing family hereby offers that artifact to the Dare County Historical Society for their evaluation and future presentation in the venue of their choice."

Marin motioned towards Cordelia and Hazel and applauded to commemorate the exchange. A flush of purpose stained Cordelia's cheeks as Eli stepped up and wrapped her in a congratulatory hug. Her camera lanyard tugged against the back of her neck as Tyde took the device and captured the moment like an able-bodied assistant. Suddenly, a tear formed at the corner of her eye as she gained her reward for bringing the issue to bear—cooperation.

An impromptu grouping of the historical society members ensued. Eli soon rose from the huddle. "The president has decided to bring the old scull down as part of the ribbon cutting event dedicating the park later this summer. I think that will add more than a little drama to our planned event."

Anna Lisa appeared on the stairs beside Tyde and she nodded at Marin with a twinkle in her eyes. "Since we're such visual creatures and seeing is believing," the artist admitted, "perhaps we should take our discovery party over to Chicamacomico for a bit of comparative analysis. Take one last opportunity to get a picture of Grandpa Walt's row house and we'll see those of you who are interested at the main station house down the road. I'll be glad to host the Historical Society officers in my Suburban, and the rest of you can follow us."

"Hallelujah and pass the air conditioning," Hazel promptly replied, which drew a rousing laugh. A delegation stepped toward the shed for a photographic farewell as Marin turned her attention to her fellow speaker. Tyde's eyes had a faraway look as his gaze traced the sound's horizon.

She tugged him down the stairs and back to terra firma. "Come ride with me." Even if the sand wasn't shifting, they weren't done—not by a long shot. But they were on their way and that had to count for something.

~

Tyde scooped up two bowls of house salad to

accentuate his story. "So strike up a victory for the home team."

Jimbo harrumphed, tossed a hot hushpuppy in his mouth, and chewed like a caveman.

"Yeah, it came off as a big victory," Marin agreed. "Now if only the newspaper article would write itself. I'll be burning the midnight oil to make the deadline for Sunday's paper."

Tyde centered the salads on a tray to help her. "Order up for Joey Tate."

Two flounder fillets spattered onto the grill behind him as Jimbo hunted the spice rack for the right seasoning.

Marin wiped her hands on the apron front and accepted the tray with a smile so brief that didn't pay any reward.

Maybe he could blame that shortfall on the controlled chaos his world seemed to be spinning into, but at least they had each other. The swinging doors reported her exit as he shifted toward the refrigerator, his focus blurred between food orders. The party of six still needed their coleslaw portions, the fries spattered in the deep fryer, and the hushpuppies hung draining.

Jimbo flipped the six fish fillets on the grill and stepped past him toward the front. Just short of the doors, the big man made a choking sound, clutched his chest, and doubled over into the dining room like a white-clad avalanche.

Surreal numbness ensued. The police officer reacted on instinct from the dining room, knelt beside the victim, and called in the ambulance. Marin held the tray like a shield in front of her as if to ward off the misfortune that arrived on her shift.

A buzzer sounded behind him. Tyde lifted the fries out of the vat and turned the fryer off. He rescued the fish from the grill, extinguished the gas feed, and managed to find take-out boxes for the works. In short order, he had the party of six on their way with supper and a rounded-off bill.

A whirl of lights signaled the ambulance's arrival, and Kyle Grayton led the crew inside. This time, the gentle giant looked more like a skilled technician as he knelt to assess Jimbo's condition. Marin tiptoed back into the kitchen and stared at him with lips trembling as he stashed the remaining coleslaw into the refrigerator. He took her into his arms and whispered sweet assurances that everything would be okay, despite his inner chaos churning a sailor's knot.

"They're taking him to Albemarle Hospital," Joey called over the door. "I'm sorry as I can be about this, Tyde. Can you lock things up here for Jimbo?"

Tyde released his hold on Marin with a cooperative nod. "We've got it. Tell Kyle I'll drive up tomorrow afternoon to pay Jimbo a visit."

"Better call and make sure he's out of ICU before you go to all that trouble," Joey replied. "Maybe you'd be more help staying here to keep things running since Jimbo's self-employed and all."

Marin untied her apron. "We can't. Not without some reinforcements. I already have a day job that's not getting done."

Tyde saw something click with the officer as he stuffed his hands in his pockets. "I've got a parasitic kid brother living off me at the beach house. How about I send him over here to chip in while you're shorthanded? You know, do us both a favor."

"Tell him to be here at four-thirty tomorrow and we'll make it work," Tyde replied.

Marin hung her head, her tiredness showing. "Talk about trial by fire. Friday nights can be brutal around here in tourist season."

The officer smiled as though the punishment matched the crime. "Let me call you if Kyle radios in any updates. It's out of our hands now anyway."

Tyde watched as the fearless defender of law and order grabbed his boxed dinner, dropped a tip, and exited out into the night.

"Poor Jimbo." Marin's resolve disappeared into a pool of pity and she began to sob.

Tyde flipped off the dining room lights as she came to him, and like taking an oar stroke toward the next trap, he pulled her in with certainty of motion. Ache mingled with pleasure and he couldn't decide which held the upper hand, as if the sensation could be separated into components. He kissed her tears and held her close while his earlier victory flashed to mind, now dampened by the fall of a larger-than-life fry cook.

~

Her gaze set on the sound, Marin wondering if her weak lamp shimmered across the bay to where Tyde lived. The laptop's keyboard clacked against the clock's movement into early morning. She paused to rub her bleary eyes with the back of her hand. Having written the lead-in for the article the day they discovered the embossment in the shed, she now had to tell the rest of the story, giving the historical society more credit than deserved for the translation of the wayside structure into historical outbuilding. At half past midnight, credit came easy to render.

She wove the quote Eli Etheridge had given her into the copy and stifled a lengthy yawn. Coastal folklore sure had a strong following across the state, and this lifesaving station mystery would raise an eyebrow or two. Worried that a reporter from Raleigh might come over to claim jurisdiction, she wondered if she should leave part of the tale untold or include vagaries instead of providing specifics. She blinked to clear her mind.

With her credibility as a writer on the line, she opted to seek the higher road of truth as they knew it. Everybody loved a mystery, so she wrote up the verification of the sound side wonder and left how the cart shed got there as open-ended suspense for the readers to decide. Filing through the photos she'd taken at the Fearing cottage and Chicamacomico, she selected two comparative close-up shots of the structure and a panoramic shot of the restored lifesaving station. With some hesitation, she included Tyde's shot of the historical society members and added a tight shot of the identification letters embossed in the wood.

When the screen filled with a close-up of the interpretive sign depicting the crew rolling out the rope cart, she stared at the profile in the background. There stood Tyde with his eyes a depthless blue and the worries of the world riding his shoulders. What in heaven's name could she do for him except love him through it? The feeling steeped from head to heart. She loved the waterman whose life threatened to disappear with the next moon phase.

"Help me help him, Lord." She saved and sent the document on for publication.

~

Tyde found his mother in the emptied library,

poring over some old papers by lamplight. He stood by the desk, waiting for her to look up and acknowledge him before he led into his news about Jimbo.

Forehead resting in her palm, she studied a series of clauses blurred of detail for the lateness of the hour. "I wish your father was here." She looked up with red rimmed eyes.

"What would that accomplish besides opening up old wounds?" he asked, surprised at her change of heart.

She shoved the papers higher onto the desktop. "Maybe he would understand this 'Fearing Exclusion' clause and let me know how binding it is. I'm about to give away his heritage lands like it's nothing. Grandpa Walt must be turning in his grave."

Tyde wiped dust from the brittle lampshade with a fingertip. "Dad could have opted to stick around and guard the homeplace if it meant anything to him. He left, which tells me it didn't matter enough."

She rolled back in the desk chair, the motion jarring her would-be tears into full blown leaks. "I'm responsible for sending him away," she confessed with a heavy sigh. "He left the house so we could live here, you and I…"

"What? He couldn't stay as a faithful husband and father?"

"He always cherished being your father, Tyde. Don't blame him for that."

"Who else is there to blame but Dad himself?" His voice squeaked like he was fourteen years old again.

"Blame me, Tyde. You're old enough to know the truth now. The dissolution of our little family was my fault, not your father's."

The skin crept on the back of his neck as something he had a vague awareness of now slithered into better light.

"In a weak moment of the flesh I betrayed your father's trust, and he couldn't find his way to forgive me. I'm not proud of it, but that's how it played out. Wade left disgusted with me, and I could never find a way to come clean about it with you."

With his eyes closed, he braced his thighs against the desk. The day's memories played back until he recalled the catty look from Lonnie's father.

"Darien Grayton?" he asked, a tone of incredulous denial raking his voice.

She nodded without making eye contact, her face pressed into her palms. "It was nothing... over in a matter of weeks."

"It ruined everything for us," he countered, unable to keep the bitterness from leaking into his words. Overcome with the need to be in motion, he tore from the room and released his anger out on the porch where he howled like a wild creature. Once the red-hot need to blame someone passed, his thoughts ricocheted on the topic of love. How could it be nothing—and everything—all at once? Pierced by the realization that he had a lot to learn, his life on the water suddenly seemed simplistic. Unaware that he sought resolution, he broke into a run and didn't stop until his feet were in the waters of the sound.

Chapter 10

Marin sat at her desk, possessing less than an hour to get the week wrapped up for the non-profit headquarters before she trekked out to Wanchese to meet the Recreation Department's assistant director. With her week dominated by the historical aspect side, her sense of fairness allotted the rec department adequate opportunity to make their pitch for the Fearing land as a park with water access. Too bad that had to equate to time spent in the field, as she didn't feel like she had a moment to spare. A pile of unopened mail glared at her from the in-box.

Hitting the 'send all' key, she electronically transferred a copy of the newspaper article to her board of directors as a matter of protocol. Lining through one item on her to-do list, she turned toward the mail and her eyes locked on her cell phone. For the second time that morning, the same idea penetrated her thoughts. This time, she allowed the thought to progress, weighing the ramifications, mostly to her privacy at the cottage. When the pro aspects finally outweighed the cons, she phoned home. What a shame the call for reinforcements had to be accompanied by dependency, as she was in no mood to babysit.

Asking for help came easier than she imagined, and before she closed the phone she had landed a deal. Her younger sister could report for restaurant duty by four-thirty that afternoon and stay the weekend on a trial basis. That would mean a manic tidy-up job in the spare room of her cottage, but the extra restaurant help would be worth it. At least she hoped so.

The land line rang and she checked the time on her computer screen before answering. Not even nine-thirty yet and the outside world needed something from her. How could everything be a time sink all at once?

She held back her frustration by pinching the bridge of her nose. "Hello, Dare County Advocates. This is Marin. How can I help you?"

"Marin, it's JD from the Daily Advance. Real quick, we received your lifesaving station copy. Hold onto something—you're not going to believe this. I sent a one-line hook out to the Associated Press and they bit on it. I'm forwarding the article along with the Fearing Cottage piece from earlier in the month to see what they'll take. I wouldn't be surprised if they use them both, combine the heart-tug of the lonely waterman with the historic revelation of the shed. Great work deserves a great pay-back, you know."

Now sitting straight up to better focus, Marin braced against her desk. "Slow down, JD. Are you saying the AP might run this in papers all over the country?"

"Yes—and pay a premium to do it," he replied. "They have a standard rate, but I think they'll bump that up if they go for the Fearing article too. Guess that makes me your broker, so I'll take the pay-out and redirect the lump sum your way. Solid newspaper work, Marin. You should be proud."

She propped her forehead in her palm. "Today must be my day to forfeit privacy. Wish I had the chance to run this by the Fearing clan, but I hesitate to re-tie the knot with the fish already on the hook. You have my permission to go with the AP offer."

"Atta girl, Marin! I knew I could count on you. You won't regret this, I assure you. No matter what, the article runs front-and-center on section one of Sunday's Advance. We may even go color on the modern-day photos. Hey, I wanted to ask if you've set a date for the grand opening of the new park. I might include that since the public may be interested in seeing the cart shed and the rowing scull part ways for the first time in a better part of a century. Good grief, I may have to come down myself. Salt air always does wonders for my mindset."

"September first, JD. That's do-or-die for my master plan, the Monday of Labor Day weekend." Marin shot a glance at the calendar under her ledger. "Right now, that master plan remains conceptual with an end-of-month deadline poking me in the ribs."

"Welcome to my world as a newspaper editor. I get a junkie adrenalin rush from it though, so ride the wave, Marin. You're doing your groundwork, the article speaks to that. I'm sure it'll all come together in good time. Trust your instincts and make your best pitch."

"Thanks for the pep talk, JD. I have to run to my next planning meeting over in Wanchese. I'll update you on the demolition at the Fearing place when the dust settles."

"No, I want a picture, dust and all, when that thing falls. But stand clear. I don't want my ace cub reporter to catch any debris when that grand dame meets the wrecking ball."

Ready to get off the line, she yielded to a relinquishment. "You'll get your photo."

"One more favor before you go. That Labor Day weekend is also 'Parole for Poverty' where we pretend to arrest area citizens for donations to local food pantries. I need a co-chairman for OBX, as the charity effort expands to the islands for the first time. Got any ideas?"

Out of time, Marin checked through a mental list of potential candidates, mostly quiet folk of non-celebrity status that wouldn't create any significant draw for the cause. Then Tyde's mother locked into her thoughts.

"Well, I met artist Anna Lisa Golden this week at the Fearing cottage. She might be willing, plus she has ties to Elizabeth City and the island. That could work out well for planning purposes. Maybe she'd be willing to donate some artwork, too."

"This is precious information. She'd be perfect. I'll take it from here."

"Call her next week late when she gets back into town," Marin added. "Gotta go, JD. Forward me any editorials that come in about the lifesaving station shed. I'll be in touch."

~

A rose garden tour could be construed as proper anger management therapy, Tyde lamented as he strolled up the slate walkway behind his insistent mother. She traced the outline of flowering foundation plants with a painter's flair, gesturing over the arched rose trellis that gated intruders out of the splendors of the owner's formal gardens in back. Loblolly pines flanked the property, lending it character despite its general lack of waterfront. Not everybody could be so lucky, he admitted, trying not to dread the waste of a perfectly good morning. His mother knocked on the front door and before he knew it, the time trap had been set.

Cordelia opened the door for her guests. "Anna Lisa dear, it's so good of you to come. And you've brought Tyde. How perfect."

He forced a smile and waved from the sidewalk, hesitant to enter the house.

Anna Lisa bent to hug the elderly woman. "Cordelia, your reputation for rose gardening knows no bounds. I can hardly wait to see the color play across your garden in the morning sun."

"Maybe I'll just stay out here and come in through the side gate when you're ready." Tyde pointed toward the arch.

"Suit yourself, son," Anna Lisa replied. "I've asked Tyde to come take pictures of us in the garden and capture the roses so I can paint them later. You don't mind, do you Cordelia?"

"Mind? I'm delighted as a hummingbird on a trumpet vine flower," she replied. As she shifted her belt to center the buckle that defined her waistline, she stepped aside to let his mother enter. Cordelia gestured toward the worn stockade fence separating her yard from the next.

"We're going to girl talk a few minutes, Tyde. Why don't you see if Hazel is still outside? She's been knocking around the yard this morning."

Tyde heard someone rummaging around beyond the gate. Curious, he stepped over to find the heavy-set woman under a floppy hat, stuffing day lily clippings into the trash can.

"Well if it's not the sweetest little lady on Manteo Island. Good morning, Miss Hazel."

She startled at first but recovered as she mopped her brow beneath the hat's brim. "Humidity's up this morning, isn't it, Tyde?" An unassuming smile graced her face.

He hung his arms across the gate's ledge and returned the gesture. "Rain by Monday may take it down a notch. Guess I never realized that you lived right beside Cordelia." His gaze scanned the neat backyard. Quaint ceramic statuary dotted well-tended flower gardens and birds fed above a bricked patio by the back of the house.

"Only for forty-five years. They moved in four months ahead of us, so Cordelia still refers to me as the 'newcomer' now and then."

"It seems like we've given her lopsided credit for flower gardening, as you've got quite a lovely spread going, too."

Her chubby arm shooed the compliment away, but her eyes twinkled to say otherwise.

"Mind if I have a look around?"

"Oh, where are my manners this morning? Please, by all means, come in, Tyde. I've wanted to tell you how much I enjoyed Marin's presentation at the Fearing cottage yesterday."

He worked the gate latch and entered, first offering a hug to the gardener. She hugged him back, sweat and all, which made it all the more genuine to him.

Hazel shifted her rumpled shirttail. "You and Marin seem to be making the most of your time together this summer."

His smile tugged to one side like a boy with a hand in the snack stash. "Yes ma'am. But with all the other goings-on, it doesn't leave Cupid much time to sling his arrows."

She beckoned him further into the yard and led him to a small shaded pool where goldfish darted under lily pads upon their approach. "Love doesn't take up the in-between, young man. You'll discover it's the other way around. Love takes up the center space, and everything else fits around it." She took some pellet food from her pocket and sprinkled it on the water's surface. In an instant, gulping fish caused the water's surface to bubble.

Fascinated, Tyde produced the camera and took a shot to capture feeding time. Such a look of unchecked pleasure filled the face of his host, he took another photo of her against her life's work—a gentle garden that teemed with life. He waggled the camera at her. "I hope you don't mind."

She waved him off and walked along a stepping stone path. Grass grew between the cracks, creating a luxurious pavement laid by time and patience.

The effect didn't escape him one bit. He regarded the flanking entourage of calla lilies interspersed with ceramic lighthouses. At the touch of a switch, she activated the sentinels and a beacon of light shown from each of their lenses.

"We used to have the local scout troops over quite a bit," Hazel said. "The kids just ate up this part. Harold's been gone for sixteen years now, but I simply don't have the heart to change a thing." She tucked into a wrought iron bench with a sigh.

Tyde knelt in front of a replica of Hatteras lighthouse. A leggy toad hopped away from the bottom of its barber pole swirl. "I guess this backyard reminds you of him, which comes back to what you told me earlier about love in the center space." He inhaled and gained a trifle of understanding in the garden's tranquility.

She nodded and removed her hat to rest in the shade. "Go ahead and look around all you want. I need to stay a spell, now that I'm down. The knees always go first, and I haven't been brave enough to consider the artificial replacements."

"No ma'am, Miss Hazel. You're one hundred percent genuine with no artificial preservatives." He stood with the camera cradled against his chest. When she motioned him away like a fly, he took a stroll to admire her handiwork. At the far back corner, he shot a frame across the planting bed, capturing the lighthouses and their weary keeper. Peace came over him despite the kitsch of the informal gardens. The place had heart, with its bird flutter, fish nibbles, and an errant toad or two. Love could flourish in such a place, which made perfect sense to him.

"Tyde? We're outside now," his mother called from across the far fence.

He closed the camera and bid farewell to his host with a kiss on her kerchief-tied head while her straw hat rested atop her folded hands. As he threw the latch, he reveled in the realization that one never knows when a blessing waits around the bend, or even behind a lowly garden gate. He doubted Cordelia's yard would feel that way. In fact, he was sure of it.

~

Wanchese reeked of sour nets, which hung everywhere under the trees that fronted slightly ramshackle houses. Certainly authentic, the fishing village stood in stark contrast to nearby oceanfront communities with piling-set mansions and condos that mushroomed from every available lot. The here-and-there tacky array of aging houses surprised Marin as she slowed to take in every detail. Lacking curbs, the yards seemed to merge with the road, evidenced by the occasional stray dog and unattended child wandering out into the opposing lane. Since her car comprised the solitary element of traffic, maybe the lack of barrier didn't matter in such a time-stand-still world. She liked the place at first glance and waved at everyone she passed.

The marina appeared on the sound side, edged by rows of seaworthy fishing vessels and shrimp boats tied at the dock. Directed to pass the marina by half a block, she cruised by at a snail's pace to get a pulse on the activity at the facility. A shrimp boat named Sally Ann poked out beyond the first dock, her nets laden with the blocky trap door required for excluding sea turtles. Apparently time allowed some improvements to be made—but only a select few. That came as a nice reminder on the eve of composing the land use plan.

Spying a county vehicle up ahead, she pulled into the first available drive and found a parking space away from the water. She wanted to walk this last portion to take in the atmosphere around the public access to deem whether it was worthy of reproducing or not. She passed a secured trash can with litter scattered beneath it. Her contact stood out on a floating dock, retrieving more trash from the water with the aid of a paddle as a shorebird flew away.

The parking surface transitioned into a concrete boat ramp without warning, so she followed it toward the water's edge, past two boat trailers parallel parked in the lot. Although no landscaping had been added, native emergent vegetation still lined the water's edge. Checking the shallows for a glimpse of a crab or even a minnow, she only saw sandy bottom with an occasional scar cut through the grass, most likely from a boat's propeller.

A sign hitched to the dock spelled out the park access rules with a list of prohibited activities. Marin decided to ignore it. Taking the higher road, she stepped onto the dock and met the assistant director halfway down its length. "Hey Randy, how's it going?"

The man added to the pile of floating debris he'd snared from the water's surface. "Chipping in with some park maintenance here, that's all. You've got to expect a little wear-and-tear on the environment when you create water access, I guess."

"That seems a shame. Maybe the real problem relates to your clientele." She kicked at a box for emphasis when a twelve-pack carton made landfall at her feet.

"Our clientele is John Q. Public, a fellow known to be messy on occasion."

"Is this similar to what you want for the Fearing land—a boat ramp and a dock?"

"Yeah, open dawn to dusk daily, a non-attended facility with an agreeable neighbor to lock and unlock the gate if we can snare the help. Otherwise, we'll send someone around.""I suppose trash receptacles are probably required by code or something… Too bad we couldn't try something innovative like trash in-trash out and have the public users take their trash home with them."

He laughed and reached for the trash bag tucked into his back pocket. "You're such a green horn," he quipped, his tone loaded with condescension. "I think the National Park Service found out that the take-only-photographs-and-leave-only-footprints approach didn't work. People tend to love their parks to death, so we have to make them sturdy and tamperproof."

"Guess I'm going to need a copy of your department's code requirements for parks to make sure I get all the components right in my land use plan. Can you send me those electronically?" She took the trash bag and held it open.

He stuffed the first load of dripping trash in to haul it away. "I have specifications for the boat launch area, too. Let me send you those along with some parking lot specs. The square footage of concrete required will surprise you, I'm afraid. We sure need that spot, though, as we don't have another access north of Whalebone Junction."

"I'm not convinced we need to cater to a bunch of powerboat users, Randy. What about restricting use to non-motorized boats? Besides preventing the bottom scour I'm seeing here, it would preserve the tranquility of the sound for all the passive users."

"Special interest parks don't serve a large enough slice of the public pie, Marin. Be pragmatic. We need to create a park for the people—all the people. You're selling out to special interest groups by trying to limit usage at the park."

"I'll tell you what selling out looks like." She lifted the heavy bag and twirled it to cinch the top. She choked a knot into place and gifted it back without a word. Under the realization that compromise didn't thrive here, she turned for the parking lot.

"I want that water access without a bunch of restrictions on it. Do we understand each other?" Randy shouted.

As she made her way off the dock, Marin turned and flashed him the peace sign, feeling rebellious and a bit tie-dyed by dated code restrictions and concrete-laden threats. She'd come up with something more suitable than a floating dock for spoiled boat recreationists who couldn't contain their trash. History needed a quiet partner, one that didn't drip gas and leak engine noise.

Chapter 11

Tyde balanced the parfait cup as his mother whipped into the parking space in front of the Dare County Advocates office. Regret tainted the visit. Insistent at the close of their lunch together, Anna Lisa now proffered a manila envelope as she exited the vehicle. He knew Marin had been up to Wanchese while they'd photographed the rose garden, so he could only hope she'd be back and receptive to drop-in company. As he pulled the door open, he exhaled in relief to spot her curvy silhouette framing the desk space.

"Hello, Marin. We brought you sweet gifts and salty questions," Anna Lisa said in her best public relations voice.

When Marin's gaze shifted his way, he gave her a slow wink and approached to slip the parfait onto her desktop.

She lifted the cup for closer inspection. "Oh, goodness. This smacks of bribery."

He pressed against the desk "Only if you can be

swayed by banana cream. Do you have time for us?"

She tore off the foil lid and nodded toward the guest chairs. Digging a spoon from her top desk drawer, she leaned back and dove in.

"You guys talk and I'll eat. Listening is what makes a good advocate—or so they tell me. By the way, how was your visit to Cordelia's rose garden?"

Anna Lisa leaned back and crossed her legs. "It proved to be a vision of loveliness that unfolded one row at a time."

Tyde snorted in disagreement and shifted in his seat to get comfortable. "I liked Hazel's garden much better. Did you know they've lived next door to each other for forty-five years? But they couldn't be more different."

Marin shook her head and dipped the spoon back into the yellow cream.

"Hazel has a fish pond, birds galore at her feeder, and a line of ceramic lighthouses along the back that really light up. I'll show you some pictures later. It's just one of those places that feels like home."

"Speaking of home, we have some official business to discuss as well, about the Fearing land," Anna Lisa added.

A dread came over Tyde, something that seemed to happen every time an inference brought his father into the subject matter. His mother produced the legal papers and turned partially into the document to a trouble spot he couldn't make heads or tails about.

Anna Lisa settled it into her lap. "This is our copy of the land title, and I'd like to read from this section numbered six point two point two."

"Let me write that down." Marin switched the spoon to her left hand and scratched the figure onto a note pad.

"Entitled 'Fearing Exclusion' this section reads: "Whereas the land described in section one referred to as the Fearing property, upon consideration of its sale or transference hereunto of ownership, a remnant of the original said tract shall remain the exclusive property of the Fearing family, its heirs or legal representatives, constituting no less than twenty percent of the original extent of the property as deeded to the owner in this initiating transaction, dated the year of our Lord nineteen hundred and seven. Retention of this exclusion shall be heretofore considered a retainer to protect the recognition of the grantee, Willis J. Fearing, to whom the land has been conferred by the Honorable Benjamin G. Pritchard, Governor of the State of North Carolina, to ensure the de facto preservation of the Fearing namesake within the County of Dare. To wit, the land retained under this clause shall be deemed the 'Fearing Exclusion' and may not be revoked or transferred under any stipulation regardless of time, so long as a legal heir exists to hold such property.'"

Dazed by the legal lingo, Tyde leaned forward and grabbed his forehead.

His mother took an audible breath to recover from the reading and let the document fold back together. With concerted effort, she slipped it back into the envelope.

Marin's face glimmered with the nuance of something positive. "This makes my land use plan get even more interesting." She stood to throw the empty parfait cup in the trashcan. "It sounds like, by legal exemption, you're required to keep at least a sliver of the property since you have an heir. That's a minimum of twenty percent that has to be retained before donating the remainder to the county. We could work that into a win-win for all parties involved with some minor scaling back of the park plans."

Anna Lisa's expression seemed wounded. "You mean we can't give it all away?"

Tyde straightened in his seat. A flashback of his dream plan came tangled up in her worries, dreams of recreation on the sound side that depended on water access to stay afloat. "This means I could still have a shot at my recreation concession."

When Marin gave a gentle nod at the mention of his goals, the whole office setting took on a surreal quality. Part of him felt resurrected as hope filled his chest. Before he could say anything else, Marin pulled him to his feet and wrapped him in a hug. It landed like a notary seal, guaranteeing his future on the water. He lifted her off the floor as if to crimp the embossment in place, compelling him to trust it could happen.

"Wade should really be here," Anna Lisa said, sounding lost and a bit afraid.

"Who's Wade?" Marin whispered.

Her breath cut a streak of goose bumps down his side, like a reactive tether to his heritage. "My father." He buried his face into her neck. "She wants my father back." When Marin's eyes momentarily hollowed with apprehension, he realized certain things fell outside of her jurisdiction as an advocate. That included things like regret, broken trust, and a pig-headed unwillingness to forgive.

~

Backing through the kitchen door of her second job, Marin steadied a dessert tray that had accompanied the arrival of her younger sister. She slid the tray onto the counter and returned to hold the door open for the rest of the entourage. Her mother entered next with bags full of salad ingredients, and her sister followed with the last dessert tray. When the half doors to the dining room swung open, she pulled a smile into place thinking it was Tyde. Instead, she set her gaze on a smaller version of Joey Tate, devoid of lawman muscle and heavily tattooed.

He froze one step in, unsure of what he'd run up against.

"Hey, I'm Marin. This is my mom Pat and my sister Maisie. You must be Joey's brother. Thanks for coming in. We sure can use the help."

Her sister giggled and lifted the lid from the tray, revealing tiny squares of frosted brownies.

He regarded the amicable teen and her sweet treats, then seemed to warm up a few degrees for the mandatory assignment. "My name's Jeremy." He stuffed his hands in his pockets. "Tyde said I'd be cleaning up the dining room."

"That's my specialty." Pat stepped through the doors like she meant business.

"Tyde," Marin called over the door, "meet my mom, Pat. Mom, this is Tyde Fearing."

He straightened from the drink dispenser and made his way over to shake her hand.

"Mom thinks her mission lies in throwing the dining room in order. She has to drive back around seven o'clock tonight, Dad's orders. Here's my kid sister Maisie, the dessert queen."

He nodded and looked back at her by the door. "What's Jimbo going to say about that, me losing control of the seafood menu to a pack of teenagers?" He slipped her a smile with the tease.

"I know what I'm doing," her sister replied, her ponytail bouncing from sight.

"Call tonight a trial run. We'll write 'Dessert Bites' onto the specials board and see if we get any takers."

Jeremy reappeared with two brooms. "I could slay that whole platter by myself." He left a broom for her mother and exited out the front door to sweep the entrance.

Maisie dug into the bags for the salad ingredients. "We're not even open yet and I've already scored a 'like.'"

Marin rolled her eyes. "Tyde, we'll prep the cold items."

"I'll come back once the ice is stockpiled," he replied. "It looks like we need clean glasses. I don't think we loaded the dishwasher last night, unfortunately."

She sensed a surge of take charge momentum. "Let me get right on it so we don't get backed up from the start."

"Hey, how'd you like Wanchese this morning? You never mentioned your impressions," He appeared over the half-door.

"Loved the quaintness of the village, hated the public boat access. We'll have to come up with something better than that because I have *no* intention of replicating that disgrace." She pulled the dishwasher door open and grimaced at the mess inside.

"Well—at least we're not shy of opinions."

Maisie unwrapped a head of romaine lettuce. "That'll never happen, not with my sis."Marin growled in disgust. "Come to think of it, the Wanchese public boat ramp looked a lot like Jimbo's dishwasher, full of gunk and in need of a double rinse cycle."

"I'm guessing you're the right operator that will leave everything squeaky clean," Tyde replied as he slapped the door.

"Optimism and teamwork—the start of a great recipe," Marin added.

"Speaking of recipes, can I load anything I want into the salad mix?" Maisie asked.

Marin straightened and glanced down the counter at the ingredients. "Go ahead with any vegetable. Hold some carrots out for the coleslaw, will you?"

"Easy-peasy," the teen replied, lining up her victims on the butcher block.

Marin found the dishwasher soap, threw a tablet into the door panel, and forced the door closed to start the machine. When she pressed the center button, it triggered a low-pitched hum and began the recovery cycle. She shouldered in beside her sister and claimed the largest knife from the utensil block.

She brandished the blade. "I'm in the mood to carve some coleslaw."

"You go girl," Maisie replied, humming something under her breath. "This place needs some tunes…"

Marin stepped toward the sink and clipped on an old portable stereo Jimbo had sitting in the window sill. She upped the volume and found a station with decent reception.

Within seconds, Jeremy's face appeared above the door, flashing a look in both directions. "Louder."

Drying her hands, Marin slid the volume control further up the scale and the kitchen took on a new energy as Maisie's feet couldn't remain still. Jeremy gave her a crooked grin of approval and disappeared back into the chore zone. Her mother came in, wet a dishrag, and went back out like a sandpiper dodging a wave.

"That goes off when the first customer walks in," Tyde called from the front.

"Aye-aye, captain," Marin agreed. Maisie shot her an annoyed glance, but she shrugged it off and tried to remember how to make coleslaw while the rock song pulverized her thoughts. Maybe she'd move her chopping mayhem to the end of the kitchen, away from the noise box and back toward her sanity. It had the makings for a long, deep-fried night.

~

Tyde's stomach ached for the late dinner more than his shoulders hurt from bussing tables and restocking ice. He kicked the screen door open and brought the plates in to Marin who lay across the tabletop resting. Settling the plate in front of her, he placed a conciliatory kiss in her hair. The moon climbed the eastern sky beyond the back porch and the night grew quiet in comparison to the restaurant's din.

"Any word from Jimbo?" she asked, her cheek still plastered to the tabletop.

"He'll be in ICU at least another day. They installed a stent and he responded well enough for them to consider demoting him to a regular room. We should contemplate going up Sunday afternoon, maybe after church. The restaurant's closed."

She sat up to regard her meal. "Let me think about it, Tyde. I have a shadow in town now, an underaged shadow that I have to bear some responsibility for."

"Maybe she could help my mom pack up the cottage. She's having a storage pod delivered tomorrow so we can stuff it full of boxes of outdated books and all. I'll do the heavy lifting later, but Maisie could help un-decorate the walls. It could be fun."

"Okay, I'll ask her. I haven't been home in a while. That might be good timing, especially since the big article will make the paper Sunday morning. What is this? Mixed grill?" She picked up the skewer and nibbled off the first item—a sea scallop.

"Call me lazy but I thought it would be quicker this way, with everything on a stick." He fingered his skewer clear of its contents and threw a button mushroom down to appease his stomach pain. "Only one more night and we can close out the week. Let's ask Jimbo what he wants us to do from then on. He's three weeks away from the big Fourth of July week. If he's not back by then, I'm not sure we can handle it."

"This tastes so good, Tyde. Let's put it on the special board tomorrow night as mixed grill skewers and try to phase out the frying pit operation. We could say the vat broke down."

"Or stick with the truth and tell the customers it's not operating. They don't need to know it's because we never turned it on." He took a long drink and glanced at his dinner guest.

"Great. Let me figure out what to do about the bread. Maisie's the baker, maybe she can come up with a concoction to replace the hushpuppies with something that won't clog up the next man's veins."

Having just taken a super-large bite that included a jumbo shrimp and cherry tomato, he could only manage a nod in response. A nighthawk appeared outside the screen and swooped on a large moth that had fluttered against the screen several times. With his blood pressure lowered a bit, Tyde relaxed and slipped off his deck shoes. "Given any more thought to that exclusion clause by any chance?"

"The acreage numbers have been swirling around in my head, but that's no way to do the proper calculation." Her face reflected the moonlight while she talked. "The whole Fearing tract exceeds nine acres, so you'll retain around an acre and a half—not exactly a country estate by eighteen ninety-two standards. But the way modern beach property is chopped up, it's a fairly workable allotment. My newest assignment will be to leave you something usable where the park won't crowd your privacy, should you ever decide to build on it."

Lost in thought as to what that might look like, Tyde finished his dinner and drained his glass of iced tea. As sole heir to the property, should that obligate him to rebuild—or would he pursue it because he wanted to? He closed his eyes and a vision of the sound side horizon came to him from a perspective right about porch level. Outside of four years of college, he'd started every morning of his life looking at the world from that angle. The truth hit home in a matter of seconds.

"I want to rebuild, Marin. Leave me a strip along the south end if you can." His voice grew husky. Maybe weariness overtook him now that his hunger had been slain.

"Of course you want to rebuild, Tyde. Your lifeblood flows with the sound waters." Marin slid her hand into his. "You'll need water access, too. Let me see what I can do on the design board. We have to give Water Strider a home port, after all."

He laughed almost helplessly, pulling her toward him on the bench to appease the tidal surge she generated in his heart. The kiss that followed tasted like sweet sea scallops, delectable and pleasing.

He rubbed his nose against hers. "Don't feel like you have to justify the continued existence of that sound strider guy from your article."

"Justifying sound strider? I don't think I'm qualified." She toyed with him as her eyes sparkled in the moonlight.

He started to beg to differ, but the kitchen door punched open and put out the moon with its artificial glaring light. He shoved his shoes on anticipating the inevitable.

"Late great party of eight has just arrived through Jimbo's front gate," Maisie called in rhythmic hip-hop. Marin moaned when he stood, so he lifted her up and brought her in walking on his feet like a giant puppet. "One more hour until closing, then we'll race through clean-up, I promise."

"You're counting the register out tonight, as math and I aren't seeing each other right now," she replied as she headed for the refrigerator.

Her needy statement made him feel lucky, as he had not been ousted yet, most likely due to his lack of significant digits. Surely they could last one more hour, even if the ice ran out.

Chapter 12

Eli Etheridge sat on Marin's front porch reviewing the land title while cradling his second cup of morning coffee. Maisie hadn't appeared out of the back bedroom yet, as they had stayed up late reading legends written about the Outer Banks. When her distinguished guest cleared his throat after a long sip, she thought he might have a verdict on interpreting the exception clause. Instead, a play of mischief reflected in his eyes.

"What we've got is some kind of collusion going on here," he hinted, tapping the paper with bent fingers. "Perpetuity clauses don't get dropped in place for no reason."

"You mean they might have been acquainted?"

"Oh, more than maybe, I'd say. The governor, by virtue of his position, is making a bestowment of Outer Banks lineage here. He's set the land aside and all the Fearings have to do is populate it from here on out. That's either entitlement, blackmail, or something else."

"Like what? Something more honorable than being a shady partner I hope. The Fearings don't seem to be the shifty type, short of making scuppernong wine in the back shed, I mean." Marin shifted her chair to face the water.

The old man laughed and took up his cup again, his gaze gravitating toward the sound as though to look back over time. "I'm wondering if it might have been a reward. Maybe Willis Fearing helped subdue a pirate ship lurking off the cape or something. I get an inkling that these two men were entangled in something way back when, and I plan to conduct some research along that vein. Should I happen upon a lead, I'd like to break the news—or at least state the supposition—during the grand opening Labor Day weekend. Could you put me on the agenda?"

She crossed her ankles, comfortable with his request. "Absolutely. I can use your research announcement to segue from history into the recreational aspect of the day."

"Want to tell your biggest supporter how you're leaning for the recreation component?"

She sighed and jiggled her cup, wishing it wasn't empty. "Randy wants the whole works, concrete ramp for motorized boats, a huge parking lot, floating dock, picnic pavilions, plus all the trash and damage to the ecosystem that comes with it. I looked at their facility in Wanchese. The entire complex seemed poorly conceived, so I wouldn't want to replicate it here. Fearing Landing should be special, a low-impact place where people come to experience the natural lure of the sound side."

"Fearing Landing? I like how that name hits the

ear. It has a dignity to it."

"Hope the Fearings think so, too, as I haven't posed it to anyone yet."

Eli leaned forward. "What if you keep the name under wraps until the grand opening?"

Her momentary consideration dipped into the lopsided grin of collusion as they came to a likeminded understanding. She nodded.

"Go your own way with the water access plan, Marin. God gave you the discernment to recognize what works and what doesn't. Put everything you have into that land use plan and I'll bury my nose trying to lend it some legitimacy from the Honorable Governor Benjamin G. Pritchard. We'll give the people of Dare County something they won't forget come Labor Day."

"As long as no one throws a monkey wrench into it." She closed her eyes to memorize the peaceful sound setting in front of her.

"It's hurricane season clear through the end of October. As Bankers, we have to learn to flex like a willow in the wind. That's the native's way of coping with what they can't control."

"There's only one native I'm concerned about. And when that cottage comes down, Tyde's going to feel like he has nothing left." Her deflated tone gave away her personal stake.

"Use Governor Pritchard's trick then, and bequeath him something that ensures his future. He has the land, so what more?" A blue and white sailboat crossed the sound beyond the channel marker and she watched it glide into the picture, towing the answer to his rhetorical question as it tacked into the wind. She blinked and envisioned a boathouse full of water strider rowboats, sunfish sailboats, and paddleboards all seeking the distant waterline.

"Isn't a boat always the answer?" she asked, allowing humor to lace her response.

"Only for a waterman," Eli replied, his gaze locked onto the tranquil blue horizon.

~

The trap had seen better days and seemed to disintegrate in his hands as Tyde worked the wire to close a gaping hole. His crabbing gig might be in its final countdown anyway, given that the house faced demolition in weeks. Too busy standing in the gap for Jimbo, he didn't have the energy to plan his own future, though nagging thoughts of Marin kept him from totally abandoning ship. He teetered across a floating barrel, shrinking from existence one second and striking out into a bold future with her the next. The conundrum rolled around in his mind like shorts in the dryer. Maybe a buzzer would sound and the mental turmoil cycle would be done.

"Tyde, there's one last box from the library," his mother said through the screen door of the kitchen.

Her footsteps trailed away as he hooked the last coil through, crimped it, and cut the wire with a beat-up pair of tin snips. "I'll get it in a minute." He carried the trap beside the front steps. Maybe he'd hit the crab line right after lunch and save some extra time for the restaurant, since the Saturday crowd would arrive in strength for the early-bird special. His glance dropped over to the POD storage unit she had ordered and he wondered how so much heritage could get deported into such an inglorious container. A sick sensation came up the back of his throat and made him swallow.

"How about lunch out on the porch like the old days?" she asked, appearing at the screen door. She soon seemed lost in thought, her gaze riveted on the sound.

"Okay by me. I'm not that hungry, but let's go ahead and eat so I can get to my crab pots early. We're expecting a big crowd tonight at Jimbo's." The clatter of a pan was his only answer as she busied herself by the sink. He grabbed another trap and examined it before tossing it over by the first one. A third trap laying at his feet had an entire seam open up which seemed like a little more work than he wanted to commit.

He pulled at the bill of his baseball cap and squinted across the sand toward the cart shed, allowing his gaze to wander over the myrtle thicket behind the structure. Whether prison or protection, the land was his. Forcing his hands to address the repair, he had the seam re-laced as his mother appeared on the porch, tray in hand.

"Lunchtime," she called, her tone light and promising. "Something you can never resist, super nachos."

Though guilty as charged, he shrugged his shoulders to squirm out of being nailed.

She chuckled as she settled the tray on a small table between the hammocks. "I'll be right back with the tea, so come on up before the flies find the food."

"Yes ma'am." He tossed the trap on top of the other two, forming an impromptu tower. Sand grated against the worn steps as he headed for the porch. He stepped out of his flip-flops into the rinse tub on the deck. A hose nozzle awaited his attention at the crab-picking station and he blasted the crustacean smell off his hands, then let them air dry.

His mother reappeared from the kitchen with a glass of iced tea in each hand, looking at him in a peculiar way.

"Is something up, Mom? You look funny."

"We need to talk over a few things… like what's going to happen here after the house is gone. Sounds like we'll still have a piece of land, according to the exclusion clause, so we ought to make plans for it, don't you think?"

He took his glass and sat at the table, eyeing the melted cheese that flexed its way over the triangular tortilla chips laden with ground beef and salsa.

"I don't have any answers."

She nestled beside him and bowed her head.

"Thank you God for today, which is about all we have left. Amen." When she looked up, he could see a storm brewing in her eyes. It didn't take long to hit.

She shoved a spatula under the nachos. "I need to talk to you about your father."

A large plank landed on his plate and he fingered the edge, not sure he wanted to hear. He hoisted a chip toward his mouth and hesitated, taking a breath. "Tell me only what I need to know," he cautioned as he stuffed his mouth full.

She placed a few chips on her plate. "I donated the land to Dare County mainly as a ploy to get your father to come back."

Tyde choked as he chewed, a sharp point jabbing the roof of his mouth.

She slid his tea toward him so he could drown his reaction. "You see, I knew they'd have to contact him eventually in the legal process, as he has to give consent for the title transfer. The letters I sent never got any response, so I had to try something else and went with the land."

Pity gave way to anger as the tea trickled down his throat, until a realization emerged that topped the rage reaction, cooling it with an understanding that he'd lacked before. He looked at his mother with new empathy and she held his gaze in wounded acknowledgment.

"You still love him, don't you?"

"Yes, I still love Wade, even after all this time apart." She traced a water drop down the glass with her fingertip.

He reached for another portion of nachos. "From my limited experience, love makes time stand still."

"Only when it's shared," she replied. "And when it's not, time drags on perpetually."

He lost himself in the lull that followed and wondered what he could suggest to close the gap between his parents. Something was missing besides his dad, like forgiveness that sped the clock hands into an eternity of separation. He had his own quagmire of emotion balled up in that division, but right now that didn't seem to matter.

"Want me to ask Joey Tate to search him out for you? He could check police records. We'd at least know where Dad is if you ever wanted to approach him."

Her eyes soon welled with tears. She eventually shook her head. The negative motion sent the tears flowing downstream.

"Can you tell me if either one of you ever officially filed for divorce?" When she shook her head, Tyde felt a flicker of hope on her behalf.

"I never wanted it to be over," she admitted with a sob. A tremble shook her shoulders and he reached out to touch her arm. She seemed frail to him for the first time, shattered by a self-inflicted wound too foolish to fully recount.

He stroked her arm. "Maybe God doesn't want it to be over either."

She balled a fist up and pounded the table with it, sloshing her glass of tea. "The house condemnation is forcing my hand…and taking away your home."

"Believe me, I've had my angry moments wondering why it's happening on my shift. But I have a glimmer of hope, Mom. Maybe it centers on that twenty percent Fearing exclusion, which holds us to the land like a lifeline."

"And perhaps Marin has something to do with that hope, don't you think?"

Tyde ran his fingers through his unkempt hair and laced them together behind his head, arching back into a stretch. With his ears burning at the mere mention of her name, he'd be living a lie to deny it now. "I can hardly think about anything else without her being right in the center of it, Mom. I'm in the crab pot searching for a way out, and her hand is on the trap door waiting to release me. I'm caught up in it, though I don't know what she sees in me."

"Oh, I do," she replied without a pause. "Honey, don't you know that you're the real deal? You're tucked away back here not letting the flashy veneer of the modern world distract you from God and his creation. I think Marin sees that Tyde Fearing. I can read it in her eyes, the way she looks at you. There's not a lot of enigmatic out there, son. She has a gift to see it, and enough heart to help protect it. But you have to let her in."

"In what?" he asked in a sharp tone, raising his arms toward the house. "My faltering kingdom? I'm heading for a fall here, Mom, and don't know where I'll land. Why should I bring her along for that downward journey? Is that fair to her?"

"What's not fair is shutting her out and not giving her the option to choose. This becomes a matter of the heart, not clapboard siding and nails. Did you ever stop to think that maybe her strength comes at the precise time you need it most?"

He allowed her question to echo from the porch unanswered as she dried her cheeks with the back of her hand. A cell phone rang through the screen door and she slid from her chair to take the call, leaving him alone to ponder Marin's strength as an anchored mooring for his shifting state. What kind of couple would they make with the woman being the stronger half? His throat went dry at being the weak link.

Minutes later she approached inside the screen door. "They want me to serve as celebrity hostess for the 'Parole for Poverty' charity over Labor Day weekend. That was JD Callahan, Marin's editor from the Daily Advance. I volunteered to be in charge of the Outer Banks outreach this year, so I'll have to cash in a few chips to get the donations flowing."

"You could always say 'no' and spare yourself the trouble."

"What would that accomplish, Tyde? I like the thought of raising money for the less fortunate. Besides, it keeps me connected to the community and that's rewarding."

"So what's with the 'parole' part of the gimmick?"

"The donor gets to have a target 'arrested' with fake handcuffs and a matching pledge request to regain freedom. Hence, they 'parole' themselves by joining in the fundraising. Save your tip money, because I plan to hit up Marin for nominating me." She laughed in threat.

"I can be pretty tough to pin down when push comes to shove," he warned.

"But not when the lock-up comes from love," she countered, disappearing into the kitchen.

A laughing gull cried on its way to the sound and he closed his eyes to stop the swirl birthed by loss of control. The urge to row hit him full force, so he stood and ran down the stairs, halting for his deck shoes and the stack of traps set to go. He tossed a trap over his shoulder, his gaze on the corner of the wrap-around porch. "Catch me if you can," he said, flinging the threat toward the condemned structure.

With the remaining traps in his grip, he balanced the load down the stepping-stones and almost made it to the road crossing when Marin's car pulled into the drive. She flashed a smile through the windshield as her sister gave a little wave. Growling, he tossed the traps toward the bow of Water Strider and stepped back to receive his guests.

Marin appeared, settling a visor into place. "Let me introduce Maisie to Anna Lisa and I'll help you with these crab pots. Come take some bread trays for us."

He met her behind the car and received the friendly shoulder nudge midstride. The hatch flew up to reveal overlapping trays of rising dough, cut and tied into knots.

"So these are un-hushpuppies?" he teased as he took the first two trays from Marin. Maisie smirked and leaned in to take the next pair.

Marin shot him a smoky look over her sunglasses. "You mean Nags Head Knots."

His gaze fell to her glistening lips and he became duly snagged. Who knew menu substitutions could be so outright tantalizing?

Chapter 13

Marin motioned to Tyde from the porch. "I'd better get going, ladies."

He hauled the last box of books out to the cavernous POD unit and grunted with its deposit. Maisie clapped from the hammock.

Anna Lisa appeared from her back room, a canvas balanced in her hands. "Before you go, I thought you might like a sneak peek at this." She set the painting against the porch railing.

Marin took a long look at the subject matter. The perspective mirrored her current view from the front porch—a railing hemmed in a rocking chair in the foreground with the sound slaying the background in a slather of vivid blue. When Anna Lisa removed her left hand, it revealed a face portrayed in profile. Even without brush strokes filling it in, Marin recognized Tyde. The timeless capturing of the artwork hit her right between the ribs. "It's priceless." Unable to look away, she reached for the outer rim, thought better of it, and stroked the weathered railing instead.

"Come on, crab lady," Tyde yelled between cupped hands.

Her gaze darted toward him and then back to Anna Lisa.

The artist's eyes softened. "You two go ahead. Maisie and I will get the baking done, and then we might run over to Ben Franklin's for a little shopping. I'll leave you a note."

"Okay, but if you're not home when we get back in, we may go ahead to the restaurant to get the crabs delivered."

"And I'll bring Maisie and the bread knots at five, don't worry. You two deserve some time alone, so let me help in my own little way," she said with a wink.

Marin smiled and gave in to the urge to hug the talented artist for her intuitive perspective. A gentle arm wrapped around her shoulders and held her for a brief second.

"Hope you can walk on water," Tyde called and turned for the boat.

She broke away with a laugh, tossed Maisie a wave, and skipped down the stairs to the aligned stepping-stones. They would be alone at last, well, until they brought the first crab pot up, anyway.

~

Tyde yearned to stop and kiss her from the first stroke of the oars. When had the skiff ride turned into a pleasure cruise? This was his livelihood, after all.

Marin looked over the rim of her sunglasses from her normal position on the overturned bucket and smiled. "The big article comes out in tomorrow's paper. Are you nervous or anything?"

"I'm a lot of things, but nervous isn't one of them."

He pushed the oars over the water's surface and dug in for the next stroke. "Why? Should I be?"

She jacked her shoes loose in the bottom of the boat and wiggled her toes toward him. They were painted a friendly pink this week. "I wrote it so the reader could form their own opinion of how the cart shed might have gotten there." She leaned back on the gunwale and drew in an exaggerated breath.

"So a few hundred folks inland will read the piece and develop their own conclusions. No harm, no foul. Looks like you'll have to try harder to get me riled." He raised his chin with the challenge.

She leaned toward him and cut him with a piercing gaze. "Now whose math is off? You mean a few hundred thousand, don't you?"

"What? Did Elizabeth City have a growth spurt or something?"

"Tyde, JD sent a teaser to the Associate Press and they picked up the article. Our historical mystery will make the Easy Living section of every major newspaper in the nation tomorrow. Sorry if I forgot to mention that chain of events before now."

The numbness started in his knuckles and worked its way up to his chest as he processed the possible ramifications.

Marin placed a hand over his. "They're paying a premium rate for the article and a small bonus for the sound strider sketch that ran earlier. The extra money is a gift from God as I'm saving to buy my little cottage, but I'll split it with you."

He lost the ability to speak as the thought of a lynch mob's noose closed his windpipe. The potential for coast-to-coast judgment so threatened his immediate tranquility that when the first cork knocked against the boat hull, he almost jumped out of his skin.

Marin lifted the oars out of the water and positioned herself beside him in the stern, freeing the bow for his crab pot retrieval.

"I…can't," he said, lost in purpose and disoriented by her proximity.

"Nonsense. You're a waterman. This is what you do." She tucked her sunglasses into her neckline and made direct eye contact. "Go get that crab pot up and I'll help you get the critters in the bucket."

"You're here to help me?" His hands clamped on her arms as though to prove the physicality of it.

She shifted closer until her knees wove between his along the bench. "Yes I'm here, Tyde. We're facing this together, no matter how many people read that article tomorrow and formulate an opinion. Nothing will change what we have between us."

"It's all that matters—what's between us—and God." He closed his arms around her back. When he pulled her into his lap, his sustained yearning merged with his immediate cry for help right about lip level. Marin proved more than adequate in her role as resuscitator as they sealed their pact with enhanced vulnerability. The float beat against the hull with every lapping wave and it seemed like a heartbeat to him, a vital connection to the sound waters below.

~

Kitchen duty absorbed Marin's every thought as she ran the night's dinnertime routine.

"Crab on the loose," Maisie shrieked, her arms flailing.

As protective older sister, Marin reached for the

longest utensil in the pottery crock and tried to apprehend the agile escapee.

The swinging doors flew open and Jeremy appeared, snatched the drying towel from the sink, and wrapped the crustacean up in it. He plunked the critter into the confines of the sink basin and glanced at Maisie over his shoulder. Marin stood beside her, mouth wide open in disbelief. He turned on the water to blast the crab. "On three, open the pot lid."

Maisie found her pluck and stepped toward the stove where Marin had the presence of mind to toss her a hot pad.

"One, two… three." Jeremy dashed toward the pot with the crab under wraps and began to ditch the fiend while her kid sister slid the pot open. In two winks of an eye, the situation resolved itself, and the teenagers stood exchanging heavy breaths, much too close for mere casual acquaintances.

"Okay, you're the hero of the moment, Jeremy," Marin admitted. "Now give her a high five and get back out there. We've got a full house tonight and they deserve prompt service."

"Call me if you need anything," he offered under his breath.

Maisie perked up and nodded her agreement with a coy smile.

The interest-loaded exchange produced a groan in Marin's throat. Teenage romance was the last thing she needed to police.

"You were awesome, Jeremy," Maisie called as he exited the swinging doors.

He pointed a finger back at her and shot it like firing a gun.

Marin knew he'd hit the target when her kid sister blushed. Maybe she should shove a wedge between them. "Hey, want to ride up with us tomorrow afternoon? You could drop in to see Mom and Dad."

"No thanks. Anna Lisa and I have plans. She wants to show me around the beach."

"Well, we might need to have an agreement about supervised dating, seeing as how Jeremy appears interested."

"Ya think?" Maisie placed another baking sheet of knots into the oven. A timer went off in the background and Marin pulled away to remove an order from the grill. She centered the fillet, heaped a pile of rice pilaf next to it, and left room for a pair of knots to finish it off. She filled the matching plate and examined the order.

Tyde appeared like clockwork to deliver it. "Switch me and I'll get our dinner going. It's almost nine o'clock."

She kissed him instead of answering and took possession of the plates, throwing her hip against the door.

Tyde pulled the refrigerator door open. "Third table on the left."

Marin's eyes adjusted to the dimmer lighting as she turned sideways to file through the jumble of misplaced chairs cluttering the aisle. As she approached the table, she recognized the patron as the younger Grayton brother who had tended Jimbo after the heart attack. The connection fell in place and she realized she had never thanked him for taking her side that day at the pier. His young date seemed nervous and swept her hair behind her ears as she set the plates down. Smiling, she gave him a moment to recognize her before greeting the couple.

"Hey Kyle, remember me? I'm Tyde's friend, Marin."

"Sure, you were at the pier with us before Lonnie ruined a perfectly good fishing outing," he replied. "This is my friend Courtney. I'm trying to fatten her up with seafood, but I don't think my strategy's working."

His date scrunched up her mouth, but soon found the humor in it and gave him the satisfaction of a wry grin.

"Maybe you've come to the wrong restaurant, as we're trying to improve Jimbo's menu with some healthier options." She picked up his glass for a refill. "Lemonade?"

"Yes, thanks. I like the bread knot thingies. Tell Jimbo I said to keep them on the menu."

"We're going up to see him tomorrow, so I'll be sure to let him know," she replied over her shoulder en route to the drink dispenser. She added an ice base and stuck the glass under the lemonade spout, watching Jeremy bus a booth clear in the back corner.

He folded bills from the tip, stuck them in his pants pocket and whisked the tub toward the kitchen doors.

As he approached, she put out her hand and stopped him from passing. "What I want from you is Tyde's tip." She nodded toward the table.

He stood his ground for a few tense seconds, then leaned the tub on the counter and produced the wad of bills. "He splits with me, so I was just taking it back to him." He yanked the tub back into his arms and leaned closer. "Now what I want from you is to date your sister."

She gave him her full attention, sizing up his earnestness in the exchange. She tried to ignore the earring and the tattoo, focusing on the sincerity of his expression instead. She pulled the drink from under the spout and slid the folded bills back under his fingers.

"Lemonade up." She stepped around him to go serve her customer.

~

Tyde cut his crab cake with the side of his fork. "Think about coming to church with us tomorrow. Our service meets earlier than yours. Besides, Mom would like to have the pleasure of your company. She offered to take Maisie from there and we can leave for Elizabeth City at the benediction.

"And I get to peek inside the beautiful St. Andrews By-the-Sea Church? What's not to like about that idea? Sure, let's do it. I'll tell Maisie tonight so she can brace herself for the early departure. I think she really hit it off with your mother today."

"Which earned me a date with my favorite crab magnet in a boat on the sound," he teased. "That could be my favorite combination—a tantalizing blend of pincer and pleasure." He slipped his bare feet over the sandy floor until they came into contact with hers under the table.

"Glad I could soften the scenery for you, sound strider."

"Uh huh. Can we consider Sunday a real date with the two of us together for the day?"

"That sounds dreamy." She wiggled her toes. A jumbo shrimp striped with grill marks soon swam toward him and he gulped it down at her insistence. "Let's take my car."

He nodded in appreciation and the back porch grew quiet except for the sound of moth wings flapping on the screen."Hope Jimbo's doing okay." He spoiled a lump of rising dread by downing a big gulp of sweet tea.

~

Marin tensed on her end of the couch as Maisie read to the conclusion of tonight's featured legend of the Outer Banks.

"And on any given night, should the weather be heading for the worse, you might see him out there, standing in the dune line and motioning all to safety, a specter of the gray man of Old Hatteras. Some say he wears a rain slicker, others have seen him in a Sunday suit, but know that he's there for your safety, not to harm you…if you dare to trust an apparition." To emphasize the ending, Maisie slammed the book closed. It made a deafening noise.

Marin drew in a pinched breath. "I don't know why, but that one always gets to me."

"Maybe it's because you have too many unanswered questions from past mysteries, sis." Maisie shrugged her shoulders. "I'm bushed."

"Let's go to bed," she replied. "I'll have to read my Bible longer than usual tonight."

"Great. That means I get the bathroom first." Maisie hopped up and headed for the back hallway. She tucked the book on the shelf as she went.

"A legend never gave us anything of value…except maybe a poor night's sleep." Marin headed for the kitchen to make sure the coffee pot was set for breakfast. With church on their schedule, she couldn't afford to run late. The unforgiving tile floor made her feet ache. "Help me, Jesus. I really need this day off. Amen." With a flick of the light switch, she confirmed the coffee pot had been set and turned to crash in her bedroom.

Chapter 14

A round-faced man with a guitar took the platform as Marin allowed a glimmer of worry to surface over her proximity to Tyde on the pew. She hadn't sung in his presence and knew her alto voice had a limited range, making little contribution to the congregation's joyful noise. It was the spirit of praise that mattered anyway, so she quelled her inhibition in an instant. Tyde turned and winked at her as the electronic keyboard joined in to spread the melody heavenward. Maisie must have recognized the popular song and perked up beside her, ready to belt out the words. She drew a breath and tried her best to come in on time.

Lyrics from a scripture in Revelations unfolded and filled the sanctuary, a strong effort for the crowd of fifty-plus attendees. Words flashed on a screen above the instrumentalists and described the throne room of God, resplendent with emerald rainbows and peals of thunder. A flashback of Roanoke Sound came to mind, its waters so serene and idyllic. How much more scenic could heaven be? Unfocused, she lost her place at the chorus.

Tyde coursed through the refrain, repeating the chant of "holy, holy, holy" until she thought the rafters might part to reveal some of that divine rainbow they'd been singing about earlier. She stretched on tiptoes, which placed her chin about shoulder height with Tyde.

He slipped an arm around her and snuggled her up against him as he shook his head and closed his eyes in reverent worship.

Love swarmed her in the moment—love for him and from him—and for God from deep within. It held a floating sway over her for the remainder of the praise time. When the music drew to a close, she found it disappointing to have to sit down.

A young minister took the podium and opened his notes with a solemn look around the congregation. Someone in the back coughed as the prolonged silence mounted the anticipation in the room. A mother hurried a preschooler down the aisle toward the restrooms.

"For everything there is a season, and a time for every purpose under heaven," the minister said, his words metered and intentional. "Which means today is ordained to mark something significant as its hours are dispelled one at a time. As surely as I stand here, I know it will mark birth and death, separation and coming together, the end of something and the beginning of something else. What I need to ask is, what will it mark for you? Let's humble our hearts in prayer."

Marin squeezed her eyes closed despite Maisie's fidget on her left side. She felt unusually close to God in the moment and allowed her petitions to drift up, open to the Holy Spirit's leading. A peace descended on her like she hadn't experienced since she'd moved to Manteo for the new job. She sensed God was marking this day in a unique way for her. A benediction rumbled from the podium and she opened her eyes.

Tyde leaned over. "I love you, Marin. Really love you." His eyes gleamed while he attempted to remain demure. A hand dropped to her side and found hers, squeezing it to seal the message.

With a fire now lit, her automatic sprinkler system shifted on to provide some relief. She sobbed out loud. Anna Lisa reached past Tyde and waved a facial tissue at her, which she accepted with relief and dabbed at the corners of her eyes to salvage her makeup.

The minister shot a glance in Tyde's vicinity. "For those of you who mark the beginning of something today, I celebrate with you."

Marin blushed, managed a smile, and picked up her bulletin to use as a fan.

"Every day should bear such good fortune that we instantly recognize the blessings of God in it. And for those of you marking the end of something today, rest assured that the almighty hand that closes one door is most capable of opening yet another."

"Unless you don't want another," Anna Lisa replied, a little too loud for anonymity. The minister turned and gave her a slight nod.

Marin held her breath and Tyde froze in place. A laden gasp rocked the pew next as Anna Lisa's dam of restraint burst, and her disappointment soon began to flow down her cheeks in rivulets. Maisie made a meek conciliatory noise and crouched to slip around her to reach the sufferer on Tyde's far side.

A throat clearing came from the pulpit microphone."Scripture tells us that God collects our spent tears in a bottle and tallies them toward our account. He is a most honest accountant, which should lend us added comfort in our distress. And without trust in God, what do any of us have? Whether standing at the beginning or the end, we have to trust His divine hand. Then we owe it to Him to make the most out of each day as we walk this journey together." A solitary whimper followed this admission and the pew grew quiet.

Marin closed her eyes and prayed for Anna Lisa, that God would know her heart and hear her penitent sobs. Before closing, she remembered to give thanks for Tyde's affectionate message which would mark her day as something truly special. She opened her eyes as Tyde stuffed the folded bulletin into his shirt pocket, a memento, no doubt, of God's mark on his day. She considered it a fairly small talisman for a man featured in newspapers across the nation.

~

Tyde jarred as the car bucked off the bridge over the Pasquotank River. A wave of astonishment washed over him when Marin slowed to turn into a gas station as they rolled into Elizabeth City. His face must have given him away as she killed the ignition and lowered his window. Before she could explain, a full-service attendant limped out to the car and opened the gas tank while singing his heart out in a deep baritone.

Marin tossed her keys onto the console. "We stopped because we need the Sunday paper, remember? You stay put and enjoy the show." She slipped out with a smile and left him to bake in the early afternoon sun while a rollicking rendition of a patriotic country song gurgled out with the gas. Traffic out of town seemed steady. The lure of rural Camden County charmed the restfully-inclined across the river's tea-stained waters.

The top of a sail appeared in the mirror and a foghorn sounded that sent crossing arms in motion as the drawbridge now yielded to the waterway's traffic. A backup of cars soon resulted and Marin appeared from the shop, paper under her arm. When he stuck his hand out for the delivery, he caught sight of a familiar structure featured on the front page. Apprehension jammed under his lowest rib. While Marin settled with the attendant, he unfolded the newspaper and read the headlines loaded with mystery from the Outer Banks. His lungs seemed to collapse. Widespread exposure was going to be more painful than he thought.

Marin dropped into the driver's seat and fished for the keys. When he glanced over from the paper to acknowledge her, she read his face and reached over to pat his shoulder. Without a word, she started the car and pulled out toward the heart of town.

Tyde leaned back with the acceleration and moaned.

Marin turned north between two outdated brick schools. "Let me read it aloud to you. I'll pull into Knobbs Creek Park and find some shade. The hospital is just north of the creek, so it's right on our way."

He reached for her and touched her forearm. "Sounds like something two carefree people would do on a date anyway, doesn't it?" He smoothed his hand over her tanned skin. The innocent caress brought her lips into a curl and somehow eased the pit in his stomach. "I trust you with the news release, as the cart shed situation would have come out, one way or another. It just leaves me feeling a little vulnerable."

"Did I mention that Eli is researching your ancestor Willis Fearing and the good Governor Ben Pritchard? Get this, he thinks they may have been buddies. Who knows that they didn't move that building there themselves as coconspirators? Anyway, he's asked to have a place on the agenda for the Labor Day grand opening to reveal his findings. Think you can wait until the end of summer to have the other shoe fall?"

He shook the paper and the Sunday comics dropped out, coloring the conversation in a humorous direction. "Looks like I don't have a choice." He cracked the funny papers open. Within seconds he chuckled at the impossible gullibility of a favorite animal character and the day seemed to fall back into favorable rhythm, even if he was on the mainland.

~

"What do you mean *no* hushpuppies?" Jimbo snarled, his hand motions restrained only by the set of IV lines and monitor links on his arms. Marin shifted her chair closer to the patient in an attempt to mollify his growing displeasure. Tyde scratched his nose in feeble attempt to hide the smirk riding the boss's reaction.

"Every dinner out doesn't have to put you one step closer to a hospital visit," she admitted, her tone soothing and calm. "We gave the patrons a new menu item, Nags Head Knots, named by my sister Maisie. Kyle Grayton dined last night and said to tell you he liked them.

Tyde pulled closer beside her as though the reinforcements were showing up. "He should know since half a dozen of the bread samplers disappeared at his table."

"Bah... Kyle eats anything," Jimbo grumbled. A nurse came in and stepped to the far bedside, checking the flow of his drip line. She knit her brow at the state of her fuming patient and gave him a stern look. Jimbo relented and flopped back limp on the bed.

"I invented a skewer combination that we throw on the grill," Tyde added. "It's been pretty popular as the special this weekend."

The dry-dock chef grunted without making eye contact.

"We serve it on a bed of rice pilaf Marin makes. No hushpuppies, no fries, no fried fillets. We don't turn the fryer on at all, as a matter of fact."

Jimbo assumed a puppy-eyed expression at that pronouncement, which left his countenance pathetic beyond measure. The nurse clamped a monitor on his fingertip and shushed him for cooperation.

Marin jabbed Tyde with her elbow. "Not that we're totally saving the clientele from calories. Maisie came up with these dessert bite things we've been selling two for a dollar. Kyle might want to testify about those too, as he tried to fatten up his skinny date with a generous cluster of them." She cocked a grin intending to lighten his mood, but she still saw a storm darkening the patient's eyes. The nurse poked a thermometer into his ear.

Jimbo shifted his gaze in Tyde's direction. "How is Joey Tate's kid brother working out?" The thermometer departed and the nurse stepped back to record the results.

"Jeremy hit the floor running and has rallied to find his pace," Tyde replied. "He may have some added incentive to be productive. Marin didn't mention how cute her little sister is. I'm splitting my tips with him and he's bussing the tables behind me." Tyde rocked back to fish a scrap of paper from his pocket and unfolded it.

"He came running to Maisie's rescue when a crab ventured out of the steam pot last night," Marin added. "I think that earned him some hero points."

Jimbo harrumphed.

Tyde shifted the paper closer. "Here are the end-of-day receipt totals for the last three days. We dropped the cash bag at the bank as we came off the beach this morning. Sorry, I didn't think about taking some out for you to use here."

The nurse removed the clamp with a snap and gave him another look that melted into something akin to concern. "He doesn't need anything here," she assured them with a pat to Jimbo's shoulder. She lifted the sheet to check his stent bandage. Somehow between the numbers and the clinical care, the giant chef managed to turn a corner and closed his eyes in contemplation.

Marin reached for Tyde's hand and he squeezed it in return.

"I... I can't thank you both enough for keeping things going while I'm out of service," Jimbo managed, his voice struggling. He turned his head to look out the window as his eyes misted at his predicament. "They're going to release me tomorrow if I meet the doctor's approval. With two weeks of recovery at home, I can come back to work by the Fourth of July."

"Don't push it Jimbo," Tyde warned in a firm tone. "Come back part-time and ease into the kitchen. We can do the legwork."

"But I need the exercise," he replied. "Can you ask your sister to come up with something red, white, and blue to serve for Independence Day?"

"Oh, I think she could invent a sugar-coated firecracker just for the occasion," Marin assured him, appreciating his receptivity. Tyde stood and pulled the receipts tabulation from Jimbo's possession and gave him a handshake to end their visit.

Marin nodded at the nurse and nudged Tyde toward the door before they could cause any more emotional trauma.

"Nice article in the paper, by the way," Jimbo said in parting. "Sorry about the Fearing cottage, Tyde. My place isn't big, but you'll always have a spot there if you need it."

"I appreciate that, buddy. Don't flinch if I take you up on it someday."

"And be sure to take your crab money out of the nightly receipts," he insisted.

Tyde paused inside the doorway and shook his head.

Marin found it sweet that the big man attempted to look after his crab supplier even from his hospital bed. "I'll make sure he cuts himself in." She gave a wave goodbye but the nurse had shifted into position, blocking their line-of-sight. Tyde wouldn't speak but she knew something was working on him.

When they came out into the full strength of direct sunlight, he turned to her to let it spill. "There he lies in the hospital and he's worried about me getting my crab money. Isn't that something?" He brushed her hair back as her cheek rested in his palm.

"Friends take care of friends," she assured him.

"And you never know when your turn's coming to be on the receiving end."

He rounded a corner of the building where his nod of agreement blurred into a hurried kiss. The day reverted back to a date once again.

~

Tyde noted his mood had greatly improved since the hospital. "Great idea for ice cream, sir." Curved concrete benches surrounded smooth-topped tables that were shielded from the late afternoon sun by a row of poplar trees. His chocolate shake quickly became a sweet addiction.

"Yeah, Daddy—another great idea." Marin flexed her tanned legs around the edge of the bench. Her dip top melted in the late afternoon sun, so Tyde leaned toward her to give it a saving lick. She giggled and held it higher to give him better access.

"You're welcome, Tyde, but call me Ron, for crying out loud."

Pat moved in next to her husband. "So, tell us how your sister's doing. Is anybody buying her mini-dessert treats?"

Marin paused to lick an ice cream leak streaming across her knuckles, so Tyde took the lead. "Everybody's buying. They sell out every night. I don't want to push her production rate, but we could move twice as many. I'm sure of it."

"I've already set a bag of replacement ingredients in Marin's car, so make sure Maisie gets them, will you?" She dug a fudge swirl from the bottom of her sundae and gave it to Ron.

"Yes, ma'am, I will." He took another refreshing withdrawal from his milkshake.

Marin shifted on the hot concrete. "Jimbo requested something red, white, and blue for the Fourth of July. Got any suggestions, Mom?" A chocolate flank of her dip top disappeared next and she hummed with the sensation of deep pleasure.

Tyde took another draw on his shake, mesmerized by her every action.

"Well, I threw in a bag of marshmallows and crispy rice cereal so she could make some bars. Drip a little colored icing across the top and you have a patriotic treat," Pat replied.

"Don't know if I could rightly share those," Tyde confessed with an impish look.

"They're my favorite, too," Ron revealed, barely coming up for a breath from his triple tower banana split. "Maybe Pat and I should pop down to the Banks for the Fourth. Got any more room for us at your cottage, honey?"

"The living room sofa pulls out, so there's more than enough room, Daddy. We could watch the fireworks together over Manteo Harbor."

"And we could lend a hand at the restaurant that night," Pat added. She locked her elbow through Ron's and delivered the next spoonful of fudge to placate any possible objection from her mate.

Tyde couldn't keep from smiling at her intuition and Marin's eyes seemed to dance with enjoyment. "Jimbo hopes to be back on limited duty by that weekend, but we could use the extra hands on deck, no doubt about that."

"Sorry we can't be back next weekend, Daddy," Marin offered.

Tyde couldn't figure out why she'd even want to

come back so soon and flashed her a quizzical look.

"Father's Day is next Sunday, but with two jobs and a deadline looming for the land use plan, I have to beg off."

Her explanation landed with a thud against his resolve, which he tried to hide behind his milkshake. It would take some further explanation why he'd completely taken that holiday off his personal calendar. Maybe he should take a stab at it on their drive back.

"We'll make the Fourth serve double duty then," Pat said, smiling.

When Ron leaned over and caught his daughter in a hug, another unfamiliar emotion surfaced in Tyde's chest. And it felt a whole lot more comfortable than a concrete bench.

Marin lifted her cone toward the middle of the table. "To an Independence Day reunion."

Tyde met her gesture with his shake and Pat joined them with a dish of chocolate-smeared vanilla. The last to ante up, Ron hoisted a plastic boat devoid of ice cream but he flashed the cherry stem between his teeth with aplomb. Pat pried it out with her free hand as they all had a good laugh at his expense.

"To a special day with my girls," Ron added as he clicked his plastic tub against Tyde's cup. "And what could be better than that?" Their eyes met across the table and Tyde caught the unabashed paternal look the man had beamed to his oldest. Instead of the dull ache he expected, it left a soothing sensation, like the world was in proper order, at least in the shade of the poplars.

~

The hammock felt almost luxurious beneath them, so Marin wiggled closer to Tyde to amplify the effect.

Sounds of Anna Lisa tidying up the kitchen echoed through the screen door as the last light of day scalloped the far horizon in waves of fading aqua. She should have been anxious about Maisie's late return from her climb up Jockey's Ridge with Jeremy, but she couldn't muster any such protective feelings. When his lips buzzed her forehead, she celebrated ending their long date day with relaxation and a tease of romance.

A motion beyond the shed's outline caught her attention as she gazed out into the falling night. Her fingers reached for Tyde and landed at the neckband of his T-shirt, where she caressed his skin. The far movement grew into a silhouette. She shifted to better see the shrub line. Maybe a deer had ventured out, but its forward motion seemed all wrong. Her fingers toyed with his collarbone as she felt the first chill of unease ripple down her back.

When the shadow stepped onto the old dune line that protected the sound side, a warning siren went off inside her head. In seconds he appeared, the gray man of Old Hatteras—looking ghostly, just like the sketch in her legends book. She tried to speak, but his threat had taken away her ability to form a word. With the omen now cast against dusk's fading light, she was bound to suffer its curse. Regret that she'd let Maisie read the godless tale flushed her like an ill breeze.

Tyde pulled against her tightened grip on his neck. "Ouch, you're choking me. You sure know how to break a cozy mood." He tried to trap her foot between his.

She swallowed to prepare for action. "Tyde, someone's in the myrtles off the corner of the shed." She forced his shoulder away to face him in the right direction. She felt the ropes tense under him as he craned to take a look.

His movement turned brittle in a heartbeat as the figure closed in on the cottage grounds. Tyde's feet found the planks and he rapidly drew her out of the hammock behind him.

She peered over his shoulder, barely able to see even on tiptoe. An invisible vise clamped down on her chest, making it hard to breathe.

"Mom?" Tyde called, his voice edgy with a quiver. "Mom, you'd better get out here." Insistent, he pressed Marin up against the cottage's clapboard siding behind him.

Her fear took a quantum leap. Trembling, her knees offered little support. A choking noise escaped her throat.

Tyde reached back and wrapped his arm around her while remaining her shield.

A buzz bothered her ears and, in a moment of clarity, she realized it was Jeremy's moped bringing Maisie back along Soundside Road.

Anna Lisa appeared and snapped the tea towel in her hands. At first she seemed distracted by the returning teens until a commanding male figure appeared off the base of the stairs. The delicate artist gasped and dropped to the top step, managing to sit rather than topple down headfirst.

Marin whispered a prayer that the folklore figure come-to-life would dissolve and give them the cozy night back. The wood pressing against her back made that scenario difficult to believe. Jeremy's headlight attempted to cut through the tension, but fell slack against the fear and went out. Maisie giggled from the roadside as they dismounted.

Marin blinked while the suited stranger removed his hat in a sweeping gesture. Added discomfort pierced her side. "Tyde?" She cuffed his arm with a strangulation grip. She needed air but couldn't find any.

The man had a haggard appearance standing there alone, the dim porch light setting the crevices of his aging face even deeper. His hollow gaze searched out the contents of the porch until it alighted on Tyde.

Marin knew, without a shadow of a doubt, that bad news had arrived. Maisie gave a playful whistle coming up the stepping-stones and a surge of protective instinct came over her. She pressed her face up against his shoulder blade and tried for resolution again. "Tyde?" she asked, this time with an urgency that couldn't be ignored. She felt him draw a breath and waited for a response. Like poison, apprehension started slaying her from the inside out. Her awareness died by increments, somehow slowing the teenagers' approach.

"It's… my father," Tyde replied in stoic reaction.

"Dear God, yes," Anna Lisa whispered.

Just when the facial similarity started to register in Marin's brain, her autonomic nervous system shifted into shutdown due to a lack of oxygen. Her knees surrendered, the ill-fated night blackened, and she slumped against the house. With only a faint awareness of the weathered planking, she slid down it to form a puddle on the porch.

Chapter 15

Tyde adjusted the wet compress over Marin's forehead as his mind raced to determine which issue should be addressed first. The teens stood by the hammock, covered with sand from having rolled down the slopes of Jockey's Ridge. His father stood behind him knotted with angst over Marin's fall due to his unorthodox arrival. Anna Lisa had disappeared into the kitchen for a glass of cold water for the fainting victim. When the screen door slapped closed on her return, Marin's eyes fluttered open. Maisie let out a little yelp.

His mother shooed him away, so he stood and gave her room to deliver the water. As he turned, he caught his father's apologetic gaze.

"I came straight from a funeral for a co-worker's son," he stammered. "Sorry, I didn't think about scaring anyone coming in through the shrubs. I took a shortcut after my car ran out of gas north of Jockey's Ridge."

While he processed the information, Maisie sobbed and tried to straighten her ponytail. Anna Lisa murmured encouragement to Marin and she took a sip of water.

"We set ourselves up for the scare," Maisie confessed. "We've been reading those legends about the Outer Banks to each other at night. The last one really got to her, the gray man of Old Hatteras. It seems so silly now."

Jeremy patted her shoulder in empathy and sand rained down.

"If Marin's going to be okay, I'm willing to go up with the gas can to get your car," Tyde offered. "Jeremy, can you give me a hand?"

"Sure thing, man. Is there a water hose I can wash my arms and legs off with before we go?" He twisted his tattooed arm and the inked anchor had been obliterated with a sand-on-sweat coating.

Tyde saw the logic in his request. "Right down here under the stairs." He slid his feet into a worn pair of flip-flops. Though he had escape in mind, he only made it to the first riser.

His father grabbed his forearm. "After the funeral, I couldn't make my peace with God over time missed with my own son." His expression wore the agony of his words. "That article about the cart shed in the Norfolk newspaper set off unrest deep inside my soul this morning. I knew nothing would bring me any peace until I got here and put an end to all this needless distancing." His voice trailed off into the vacant vacuum of suffering

For the first time, Tyde felt a flicker of recovery inside his chest. "Then I'm glad you came back," he managed, his lips drawn tight to heel in the hurt.

"I'll be all right, Tyde," Marin said weakly.

Jeremy slid out and joined Tyde on the steps. His father shifted as though to join the rescue team.

"Can you stay, Wade?" Anna Lisa's soft request held a beggar's tone from where she knelt on the planking.

He regarded her for a silent second, shouldered out of his suit jacket, and nodded to dismiss Tyde. The car keys jangled with the exchange.

Descending the stairs, Tyde turned toward the water spigot and caught a glimpse of his father kneeling beside the hammock to embrace his mother. The sound of running water filled the night as Jeremy splashed his way toward clean. Tyde let it transport him off the sand yard to a place of sturdy support. He needed rock beneath him right now anyway, not shifting sand.

~

Marin turned the compress over in hopes of finding a cooler side. "Maybe we should have eaten real food for dinner, not ice cream."

"You're working too many hours dearie," Anna Lisa replied with a knowing tilt of her head. She now sat in the chair Wade had pulled alongside the hammock. Maisie sat on the porch railing where she tugged on the ropes of her sister's recovery bed.

"The restaurant shifts are taking a toll," Marin confessed. "Plus, the end-of-month deadline at work has me quaking in my boots. I truly need to focus on the land use plan if that Fearing exclusion clause is going to have any bearing on the outcome."

Wade reappeared through the back door. He had changed into shorts and a T-shirt, which made him look even more like Tyde. "What exclusion clause?"

"In the land title," Anna Lisa explained, "there's an

exclusion clause that mandates the Fearing family retain no less than twenty percent of the original acreage. It's a forever sort of clause, like the governor was solidifying the Fearing family's existence on the island for all time. Did Grandpa Walt ever say anything about it to you?"

"Not in that respect. He did like to say 'this is Fearing land' as though we should consider it an honor or something. And I always did, as a matter of fact."

She shifted in the chair to face him. "Do you forgive me for wanting to donate it for public use?"

Marin looked between them to catch any nuance that might help her plan the outcome.

Wade swallowed and shook his head. "No forgiveness needed. I think it's a noble gesture and should have been thought of before. Maybe that's a reflection of your generous heart, Anna Lisa, which is a silver lining to this whole ordeal. The public will gain a treasure, for sure."

"Oh, Wade, you're giving me too much credit," Anna Lisa replied. "It was a shot in the dark, really. The whole time I hoped and prayed you'd come home and help me with it."

"And I did come back, didn't I?" The gleam in his eyes spoke of something more.

When she raised a hand to touch him, it stirred Marin's heart. Ever the softy, her kid sister sniffled from the railing. A detail came to her and she wanted to share it. "Tyde requested the southern flank, if at all possible, sir. If that location suits you, I'll pursue that orientation for the land use plan. I'm trying to protect your family's water access, but the Recreation Department thinks they're entitled to the whole shoreline.”

“Sounds like you’re trapped in the middle, from what I’ve read.” A tight laugh chased his response.

She finished the water and handed the glass back to Anna Lisa. “That’s my job as lead for the Dare County Advocates organization, but it does feel like I’m being used as a punching bag now and then. I think you two should stop by the office in a couple of days, so we can work through some of this on paper. It would be a tremendous help.”

“I’ll postpone my going back to town given this latest… turn of events,” Anna Lisa said. “What if we come by Tuesday morning?” When she raised her brow, Wade nodded his consent.

“That’s perfect for me,” Marin replied. “Now, could I ask for a little nibble of something before I have to drive back over to Manteo?”

“I think Maisie and I had some leftover chicken wings, if that sounds good,” Anna Lisa offered.

When Wade’s face brightened, Marin realized she wasn’t the only one who’d skipped dinner. The camaraderie felt pleasant, especially from her state of weakness.

Wade smiled as lines crinkled from the corner of his eyes. “How come the end of the road always seems a little bit like heaven?”

“Why, it must be because angels frequent the kitchen,” Anna Lisa teased back, glancing over her shoulder with a look meant only for him. Wade hung his head and rubbed his eyes.

Her hammock stopped swaying. “Do you think I could de-sand myself like Jeremy did?” Maisie generated a small sandstorm by releasing her hair band.

"Try the solar shower around back," Anna Lisa replied through the screen door.

"I'll trip the porch light for you, honey," Wade added. A hand on the rail, he walked into the darkness like he knew the place by heart.

Marin closed her eyes and tried to squeeze the weakness from her system. The hammock hugged her frame, but she felt something more, like God's hand was cupping her in protection. Empty on the inside, she sensed his abiding presence like a breeze off the sound.

~

A storm flickered lightning in the distance as Tyde laid awake well into the night. He wished Marin had let him drive her back home, but she insisted that she was up for it. Where could he draw the line of dependency between them? He certainly felt the attraction drawing them together, but couldn't seem to figure out the separation angle. He closed his eyes and envisioned her passed out on the porch, helpless and overwrought by the day's events. Maybe he should have done something to lessen her load, like offered to drive the return trip.

The restaurant came to mind, so he tried to think of a way to make it work without her help, but the scenario seemed bleak at best until Jimbo's return. Plus, they spent most of their time together there. A fear lurked deep inside that he would hardly get to see her at all otherwise. Dinner together with a stolen kiss or two had become a staple of his summer. He should ask Marin what she would change, if anything.

He overheard his parents still talking out on the porch, their voices hushed by the lateness of the conversation. Every now and then his mother would laugh, punctuating their discussion with hope. Their reunion seemed dreamlike to him, and he finally recognized it represented an answer to prayer. His mother's crumbling façade at church evidenced that the current rift had to end. Leave it to the God of the universe to bring it all together in such an unforgettable way. For his part, he was ready to trust again, and more than ready to have his father close by.

When his thoughts drifted to the exclusion clause, he realized for the first time that there might be another Fearing eligible for a share of the twenty percent. Would that leave him half if they split it fifty-fifty? Shaved down to three-quarters of an acre, would the original land grant seem like such an adequate heritage after all? And would it be enough to keep him on the water? He turned on his side away from nature's light show and released the worry heavenward with a moan. Sure, God knew his heart, but would he care enough to keep his ankles wet?

~

Marin slipped to the breakfast table only to find a stack of pancakes waiting for her there. Her Bible sat open to the book of Psalms as the microwave sounded.

Maisie appeared through the back door with a coffee carafe in her hands and stopped by the microwave to retrieve the syrup. She delivered them both to the table and crossed her arms, staring at her. "I need to do more of my share around here."

Marin couldn't have been more surprised and even pinched herself to make sure she was truly awake.

"Stop with the questioning look. You scared the bee-gee-bees out of me last night. You have a day job and I don't, so I should take up more of the slack around here."

"Listen, I can handle this," she replied in defense.

Maisie poured the coffee, but didn't change her tart expression.

Marin inhaled and gave the offer further thought. "Well, maybe if you could keep the kitchen up, I would appreciate it. I can't get you to the restaurant any earlier, so you'll have to do your baking here." She nodded to the supplies their mother had sent to accentuate her request. "If you find a receipt in the bags, keep it for me. It's only fair to get reimbursed for our direct expenses. We'll have to negotiate the labor, or give you a payout for the desserts and bread knots. Think about it." She poured syrup over her stack and dug in.

Maisie unpacked the ingredients. "Mom's suggesting I make crispy rice treats, isn't she?"

"Yeah, with icing that's red, white, and blue. Jimbo requested something patriotic for the Fourth." She sipped her coffee and let the robust blend wash the pancakes down.

"That's pretty low-brow," she replied as she lined up the packages.

"But everybody loves them, Maisie. Please make a batch, at least for Dad."

"Are they coming here for the holiday weekend?"

"Yes, I never got a chance to tell you. We'll miss Dad next weekend for Father's Day."

"But now Tyde gets *his* dad just in time for Father's Day. Funny how that worked out."

"Hey, about that legends book we were reading."

"I already threw it out. How about we make our own legends this summer together on OBX? It has the makings for a real blockbuster—without the infusion of weird."

Marin stuffed another load of pancakes into her mouth, wondering when her sister had gotten so smart.

Maisie turned from her brief rummage through the cabinets. She produced a star-shaped cookie cutter and got a gleam in her eye. "Ta-da. Look at this."

"Star-shaped crispy treats?"

The teen baker nodded to seal the deal. "I'll swizzle them with some colored icing and we'll offer Jimbo the stars-and-bars for one over-the-top patriotic dessert platter."

"Way to go, kiddo. Hey, be sure to enjoy yourself along with all the work," Marin cautioned. "From the looks of things last night, you and Jeremy have started doing just that." Her comment reaped a cute smile in payback as she stood to get ready for work. Maybe rolling down Jockey's Ridge would seem like a piece of cake compared to the uphill struggle she faced.

The star-shaped cookie cutter prompted her creativity toward resolution. A geometric cut-out would be perfect for defining the Fearing exclusion, and then she could plan the park beside it. What shape would serve her best hadn't surfaced, but she had a drafting table waiting to help her settle on that representation. "I'll be back home at four-thirty. Can you be ready to head out for restaurant duty by then?"

"No problem, sis. I'll hatch a batch of knots and be sitting on go." Maisie drained the coffee carafe into her pink flamingo cup.

Marin glanced around the kitchen and took in her flock of shocking pink. The wackiness of it all put her in a high mood to face her day. Maybe that was the syrup talking, but whatever the origin, she sure needed the boost.

Chapter 16

Tyde made a game out of waiting for the toaster, only because it gave him a way to occupy his time. A chair scuffed the floor behind him. "Let's tackle the exclusion clause this morning while your mother sleeps in," Wade said. "I think I scared half a day off her life last night with my sudden appearance."

Tyde couldn't let his comment fall without sliding him a knowing smile. He claimed the bread when it popped out of the toaster and fended off his father's weak attempt to confiscate it by jabbing his elbow at him. Noticing the legal document on the counter, he opted for the margarine spread instead. "Not to mention knocking the breath out of Marin, making her black out." He pulled the flatware drawer open.

His father amicably reloaded the toaster. "Well, maybe her protector could assume half the blame, as he pinned her against the house pretty tight." He reached for a coffee mug in the overhead cabinet.

Tyde snickered as he lathered his toast with butter.

"Guess I'm a rookie at that sort of thing. At least I curbed my first reaction—to bolt right off the porch."

His father nodded in concession as he poured the mug full of steaming coffee.

Tyde grabbed a peach from a glass bowl by the sink.

"You learned in seconds what it took me twelve years of wandering in the wilderness to understand— that love doesn't run away. I hate carrying around all the regrets that come with being gone from here, but putting you through this condemnation scenario by yourself seemed too far beyond the bounds of tolerable for me."

Tyde headed out the screen door. "Maybe the land is the Fearing blessing after all. I've sure needed some level guidance on where to head from here."

Before the door could shut completely, his father shoved it open, balancing his dry toast across the steaming mug with the document under his arm. He used his foot to keep the door from slamming to preserve the morning's peace. "For the benefit of all Fearings to come, let's hope the two of us can figure this one out." Wade settled beside him at the café table.

When they both glanced involuntarily at the sound before centering their attention on the food, it struck Tyde as a bonding moment. "Looking ahead is all we can do from here, and maybe forget past hurts to make the present count." He bowed to pray and when his head came up, his father's eyes shined at him with admiration.

"How I missed all of this."

Tyde let him soak in the scenery while he launched an assault on the innocent peach. Before he knew it, he held a stringy pit and had juice trailing down to his elbow.

"You'll need to give me some time to make the adjustment, son, because when I look at you, you're still fourteen."

"Believe me, I didn't want to grow up without you. When things got to tough for me to figure out, I escaped to the sound where the people pressure didn't seem to exist."

Wade wrapped his hands around the mug. "I remember eluding your grandfather in a similar manner more than once. The sound doesn't pass judgment on a man. It lets him be who he is."

"Marin says I'm a waterman. She calls me sound strider, like I can walk on water or something." He glanced at the shed thinking she must have arrived at work by now. That little wooden rectangle would be at the center of everything she drew up today, worthy or not.

"Are the two of you in love?"

Tyde fingered a slice of toast and gave it some thought. Awash with the whole emotional wave, he knew he was in deep. "A pretty strong current is carrying me along. It's my first time, because I've shielded myself. We met when she showed up late for an interview about the cottage demolition and I let her into my boat. I couldn't take my eyes off of her the whole time."

Wade nodded. "I met your mother at a rally at the foot of Jockey's Ridge in the classic 'Save Our Sand Dunes' movement. She was radical in those days…gorgeous and well-meaning. I echoed her enthusiasm for the cause and asked her if she'd ever seen the back set of dunes tapering toward the sound. We met at dusk for the private tour and ended up with our feet in the water. I kissed her that first night right then and there on the edge of the sound. They ended up raising the money to protect the dunes and I got a girlfriend out of the deal. That proves life on the land can work together for the common good, doesn't it?"

"Nice take-away, Dad. I hope my story turns out as romantic when my kids hear it. Marin makes me more than I am, if that makes any sense. I feel like I'm hiding out and she sees so much more. I don't know. Am I setting her up for disappointment?"

"Follow your heart, Tyde. I know losing the house is a real blow, but you have a chance to start something else with greater potential than your heritage dealt you. We have to stay positive and read the fine print to make the best plan."

"Section six point two point two."

Wade flinched and flashed him a questioning look.

Tyde nodded toward the document and buried a piece of toast in his mouth.

"Ah yes, the Fearing exclusion." His father reached for the nearest dog-eared corner. "Excluded to stay put...now that has an ironic ring to it." A laughing gull cried as it flew toward the sound and they regarded one another over the residual crumbs of breakfast.

~

Marin flew through the e-mails and deleted them in sections like deadwood on her morning. She had to be productive and guard her time wisely, which meant no sidetracks and focused-forward work. What looked like an insurance ad came up next and her pinky stretched for the delete key, but accidentally hit the home key instead. Giving it a second look before launching it to oblivion, the words "small business grants" rose into focus. She froze her pinky.

The State of North Carolina offered to nurture emerging entrepreneurs by making setup grants available that led to low interest loans for future endeavors. Tyde's sound-side concession popped to mind and she scanned for more information. Clicking on the link to apply, she stared at the fairly simplistic form that filled the screen. Maybe she'd download it and share it with Tyde during dinner break tonight. She hit the print key without a second thought, and the sheet rolled off the printer behind her.

Saving the e-mail into a separate file, she worked down the other trifling entries until she came down to a listing from Eli. She sighed while opening it, worried that it might be bad news. To her great relief, his one-liner read, *Making progress on the Governor-Fearing link. Think you'll like the outcome! E.* She smiled and gave up on the computer, opting for the drafting table instead. She flexed her legs and gripped the desk edge like a runner warming up.

"Time to create an outcome everybody will favor. Lord, show me how to work this out." She stepped toward the conference room, uncertain. A glance out of the glass front door reminded her of the beautiful beach-worthy day she wouldn't get to enjoy outdoors, another small sacrifice for a work of appeasement. The land use plan had to come first.

~

The breeze riffled through the bound pages Tyde held in his hands.

Anna Lisa pushed the screen door open. "What am I

missing out here?"

Wade met her gaze with an intriguing look. "We'll end up with a smidge less than two acres for the family. That's plenty of space to throw up a new cottage or two."

All Tyde could do was scratch his chin stubble. "You know how many crabs that would take?" Wholesale unease prevented him from letting the dream take flight.

His father squeezed a wink at his mother. "Oh, at least a season's worth."

She pivoted and disappeared into the kitchen.

Tyde heard the coffee pot making its way through another sequence of brewing before too long.

Wade arched his brow. "My assets are liquid. I sold my house in Norfolk last month."

Tyde drained the last of his orange juice and recognized a palpable separation between their assets. "That's your money, Dad. Rebuild with it for yourself—if that's what you want."

"What I want depends a great deal on how your mother and I come to terms. She lives in Elizabeth City and has a thriving art studio there, plus an adoring fan base to entertain. Me, I'm a plain sound-side recluse like yourself, looking to come back and make a home where there soon won't be one."

Thinking of twin cottages, Tyde realized they might need to coordinate efforts. "Marin needs some input before her end-of-month deadline. If we're going to be any help to her, maybe we should determine whether there'll be one house or two. If we're not careful, somebody could lose their water view. Remember, we're up against a greedy Recreation Department for linear feet of shoreline."

"I'll help Marin as much as possible, but Anna Lisa and I have to make some decisions first," Wade replied in a resolute tone.

His mother appeared with her morning cup of coffee and a bowl of granola, laced with peach slices. She sat down opposite them. Wade reached over, stole a peach, and plunked it into his mouth. Anna Lisa smirked in response.

Tyde rose from the table. "You two need some time to talk, so I'll get busy with my day's packing assignment, Grandpa Walt's old bedroom."

"Wow, talk about a museum. I might like to see some of that." Wade reached for another piece of fruit.

Anna Lisa turned the spoon upside down and pretended to pop his knuckles with the eating utensil.

Tyde snickered as he stepped away. "I'll leave some of the more interesting stuff out for you to see, but something tells me you'll be out here awhile yet. Don't forget you promised to make the crab run with me this afternoon, Dad."

"Oooh," Anna Lisa cooed, mouthing the rim of her cup. "Making plans to go out on the water. That'll officially christen your return to Nags Head."

His father held a sheepish grin for an instant, and then gave him a nod of confirmation.

A major work of reparation was about to get underway on that rickety porch, but it sure didn't need his five cents of contribution. A genuine by-product of that original heart trust, Tyde knew his place, and had hidden there many times. The screen door to the bedroom wing popped closed behind him as he gave the idea of brushing his teeth some meaningful consideration.

~

Marin sketched the property boundary for the Fearing tract on a thin vellum overlay, using care not to shift the aerial photograph beneath it clamped to the drawing table. Endowment from the governor notwithstanding, the whole plot took the shape of a short-shank Christmas stocking. The bare sand inside the right-angled curve of Soundside Road gave the appearance of a heel patch, the kind that made a sock monkey smile. From the northeast corner, pines and wax myrtle stippled the aerial like eyelets with shoelaces down the stocking's length, ending behind the historic shed. It occurred to her that she should sketch in that fixed feature, so she picked up her straight-edge and traced its delineation onto the map. With the stroke of her pencil, she proved that the least feature on the landscape can become its greatest attribute.

To gain perspective, she leaned back, exhaled, and squinted with the hope some magnanimous plan of division would appear. Under such enlightenment, she could slice up the parcel with acumen. But problems were evident from the get-go. If she defaulted to keep the native vegetation, the historic park would be restricted. If the boating access took the section of shoreline off the stocking's bottom, Tyde's new residence would be left high and dry. And where could she place the requisite parking lot to meet code while hiding its concrete lack of charm?

A sip of water and a short plea for help heavenward helped reset her priorities. She had to make the components work together. The cart shed was set in place. It couldn't be moved again, given its age. Every other component could radiate from there, even Tyde's allotment.

The Fearing exclusion came to the forefront of her mind next and she reached for the planimeter tool to figure out how much one and eight-tenths acres would represent. After making several pencil marks along the toe of the stocking, she traced several variations of the perimeter along the parcel's southern flank until the total came out a shade under two acres.

When it occurred to her she had left out the waterfront access, she backed down from the cart shed and included a third of the shoreline instead. With a total of one and nine-tenths acres, she began to sense some satisfaction and darkened several of the hash marks. Eraser crumbs obliterated the trial boundaries.

Grabbing some scratch paper, she tore it into sections and began writing component names on each piece. *Cart Shed* and *Fearing Property* found ready locations on the draft map. *Boat Ramp* waited for assignment beside the map and was soon joined by *Floating Dock*, *Parking Lot*, *Nature Trail*, *Historic Site Access*, and *Playground*. Before she dropped the pencil, something else came to mind, a feature she'd been designing mentally for some time. She marked the last scrap of paper *Boat House* and lined it up with the others.

Marin lifted the overlay and stared at the aerial in a focused attempt to read the land and make the appropriate land use to match. The bare sand heel kept staring back at her, so she looked over at the collection of unclaimed features and gave each one some consideration. Too exposed for a safe playground and too far from the water for the ramp, one remaining choice became obvious. Given one-way flow of traffic with separate entrance and exit, the parking lot would flex into the bare sand heel area nicely. Randy had asked for fifty spaces for the park, but that was well above code. Taking an automatic twenty percent reduction to match the acreage reduction due to the Fearing Exclusion, she settled on forty spaces and scribbled a note to research the spatial requirements to lay out the lot more precisely. With any luck, none of the myrtles would have to be bulldozed. She lowered the drawn map and sketched a square of parking inside the curve of the road.

Wade's grand entrance over the relic dune line last night popped into her mind next, and she surveyed the aerial to examine his route. It occurred to her that a foot path leading east out of the parking area could turn and parallel his approach southward, eventually leading to the cart shed while doubling as a nature trail through the shrub thicket. She traced the dark signature of the myrtle stand onto the map overlay and laced a meandering trail through it, popping out in the vicinity of the shed. Public access from the north would protect Tyde's privacy while serving the public well. It fit with the natural topography as features began to fall into place.

The solution generated a rush of enthusiasm, fueling enough adrenalin to tackle the remaining aspects. She needed something neutral to buffer the historical site from the recreational activity, so she fingered the playground piece and dropped it into what was now Tyde's side yard. Nothing but sand existed there now, allowing room for design freedom to build a rambling fort structure for the kids. Maybe if she could style the kids' climber after Chicamacomico, Cordelia Baum would keep her hissy fit over its proximity to a minimum. She made a note to print out a picture of the lifesaving station

The two water-linked features remained for positioning. Marin took a hard look at the available shoreline. She marked out a third of the linear footage for the Fearing family. Nudging the boat house paper to straddle the one-third mark, she drew in a loop road for non-motorized boat dropoff and sketched in a public waterfront ramp. Lining the east flank of Soundside Road with a picnic area to offset the boat loop and transition toward the playground area, she stopped and surveyed the amalgamation with a critical eye. Fearing Landing had just taken form, rudimentary though it was. Better yet, she already sensed a personal attachment to it.

~

Tyde offered his father the power position and stepped into Water Strider's bow.

Wade took command, centered his frame on the stern bench, and reached for the oars as though they were sacred.

Tyde turned the bucket over, assumed Marin's usual position, and soon gained a cramped respect for proportional space. As he shifted the anchor line out of his way, he glanced out over the sound. "So, how did negotiations go back there on the porch?" He skimmed the water's surface with his fingertips and waited.

His father swept the horizon with his gaze and seemed to give his question the requisite consideration it deserved. "Let's call it clear skies to occasionally cloudy, but I think there's a fair chance of aligning air currents by nightfall."

Tyde nodded in relief, but no amount of biting his cheek could keep the boyish grin from erupting.

Wade's eyes twinkled under his cap bill. He lowered the oars prematurely to splash Tyde where he sat in the bow.

He laughed, recognizing the taunt. Not to be a solitary victim, he scooped out a handful of water to retaliate. Before a herring gull could open its beak to squawk, a full-fledged water fight had begun. He *was* fourteen again, and it felt unbelievable.

Chapter 17

Marin drew a line of pom-poms around the roadside perimeter of the parking area to simulate a landscape planting. Tyde had really pressed her for details last night at the restaurant, but she hadn't wanted to spill the beans too soon. His parents had pledged to stop by this morning, so she made herself address the presentation quality of the draft map. After easing a few angular boundaries, the components seemed to mesh with a snug fit.

A wide band of blank space above the donated tract boundary offered her room to place a header bar and she thoughtfully boxed in the block letters spelling out "Fearing Landing." She had just aligned a fairly decent letter D when she remembered that Eli had suggested they keep the park name under wraps. So far, it read "Fearing Land." She could easily add a noncommittal descriptor to draw everyone's attention away. Deciding for script, she scrolled out "Park Project" beneath the nameplate. She surveyed the effect and thought it came off distracting enough, though she could hardly wait to see Tyde's expression when they announced the real name.

To sketch in the diorama of Chicamacomico Lifesaving Station next for the children's climber in the playground, she pushed back and went to retrieve the print-out she had downloaded. When she scooped it from the printer's tray, a second sheet of paper came with it. At a glance, she recognized the small business grant application. Deflated by the feeling of having dropped the ball with Tyde last night, a teasing idea wiggled into her mind.

What if this could be part of Tyde's surprise at the grand opening park dedication? She could file for the grant and not be in too far over her head, if she could get help with some of the details. She didn't know much about starting a boat concession, but she was about to receive an office visitor who might. Her blood ran hot with the prospect of giving Tyde a head start on his big dream, but what if she bungled it in the process of pulling it off? With the application front and center on her desk, she returned to the conference room and sat down at the drawing table with purpose anew. After all, she had a miniature lifesaving station to create.

~

Tyde straddled the shoreline with one foot in Water Strider as he wiped down the hull from sand the anchor line had dragged inside. Late morning already, the sun meant business and the water seemed to expand with steady ripples against the shore. A vehicle's brakes squealed and he looked up to find a Dare County police car nosing down the sand bank, angled off the road. In seconds, a beefy officer took shape across the hood, pulling at his utility belt.

Tyde dropped the towel. "Hey, Joey. What brings you out our way?" He swished his hands through the lukewarm water and dried them on his shorts. Back on land in two steps, he headed toward the visitor.

"Looks like the tide is out today," the officer replied, his large forearms braced against his hips.

Used to the name tease, Tyde brushed it off and extended a hand, hoping the stop was all pleasure and no business.

The brawny man took his hand and jerked him around good-naturedly. "I hoped you'd be out when I patrolled by today, so I could thank you for turning my little brother into a human being I can finally stand to be around."

Tyde flashed his palms up to deny responsibility. "Jeremy's a good kid. He seems to be looking for an influence to give him some direction, that's all. Maybe a little hard work and steady tip money will be incentive enough, who knows?"

Joey peeked suspiciously from under the rim of his hat. "You didn't mention the sway of a pretty girl, Tyde. Now don't go telling half-truths and expect me to buy it."

Tyde pulled his shirttail loose and wiped the sweat from his face. He hooked a lopsided smile and glanced back at his longtime friend. "I'm caught up in the same power of sway, so don't expect me to go ratting Jeremy out. Besides, Marin trusts him, and she had ultimate responsibility for her sister this summer. I've got my eye on Jeremy and she's watching Maisie. Between the two of us, there's some level of accountability. Guess that's more than we had when we were teenagers."

"Which might be why we're having this

conversation," Joey admitted with a throaty chuckle. He kicked at the sand and shifted his gaze out over the sound.

"Jeremy asked Marin if he could date her sister, so at least he's trying to approach it honorably. Her parents are going to work in with us over the holiday weekend at Jimbo's, so he'll have her daddy's attention soon. That should be intimidating enough."

"How's Jimbo doing?"

"Came home yesterday, but he's weak as a lamb. I told him to take it slow coming back to the restaurant. He's pig-headed but this episode's really got him listening, I think. He may pop in over the weekend but he can't have any of our fare—except the rabbit food portion."

That drew a chuckle from the lawman, but the effect didn't last long. His face fell serious. "Tyde, something's up with Bushwhack that's not too kosher. The captain has a stake-out planned at his place in Wanchese by the end of the week." The officer's chin dropped to his collar and he shifted his stance. "Got a bad feeling about how this might play out. It's never easy when you know the face your gun gets pointed at."

When Joey turned his gaze directly on him, something unsettling pricked the back of Tyde's neck. "Bushwhack is choosing a dark road, Joey. You two were on a collision course from the start. Remember how he tried to make his home base the top of the high slide in elementary school? You went up there to free it for all the rest of us because you were the only one of any size who could stand up to him. And you had the guts to confront him."

"Earned me a nice set of cracked ribs when he

decided we wouldn't be taking the slide down to the ground that day." A trace of impish grin flickered up his cheek.

"My point is you've always stepped up to do the right thing. Bushwhack is on his second chance anyway, and should know better than to push the limits. I'm none too happy with him myself, after the stunt with Marin at the pier that night."

"So *now* you feel the need to protect? That's been my job twenty-four seven. It wears a man down." Joey's voice sounded weary for the early hour.

"I'm a simple crab trapper, buddy. I couldn't do it," Tyde said. "My hat's off to you for doing the dirty work at the rub of good and evil."

"Watermen can't be weighed down with guns, leastwise you'd be a pirate in my estimation," Joey replied.

Tyde cracked up with the analogy. After a cleansing belly laugh, he tucked his hat deeper on his forehead, unable to let the reference pass. "Aarrrgh, me great-grand pappy may have been a thief with the cart shed, but I'm walking the straight-and-narrow in hopes they won't be keel-hauling me bones for it!"

A weight fell off the officer's shoulders as they began to shake with laughter, and he finally swiped his hand across his face to reveal the old buddy Tyde recognized. "Thanks again for taking my brother under your wing. It means a lot to me right now." Joey turned and headed for the driver's side of the patrol car.

"No problem. And now that he knows where I live, maybe I can get him to come out crabbing with me. You know, lend a hand with real men's work."

Joey laughed, pulled the door open, and dropped

into the seat. "Jeremy usually doesn't wake up until three o'clock in the afternoon. You wouldn't want to deprive him of his beauty sleep, now would you?"

An image of the rough-cut, tattooed teenager came to mind and Tyde shook his head like that was a no-go zone. "Let's see if his crazy-for-Maisie phase will modify his internal clock a bit without us having to use brass tacks to get the same result."

"Man, you do have it bad, don't you?"

"A regular prisoner of love." Tyde crossed his wrists like a captive. The patrol car inched out of the sand and he tossed a wave as Joey's face disappeared behind the tinted glass. Drop-by visits registered as a sign of true friendship, and he felt all the richer for the exchange. If only a troublesome sandbur called Bushwhack hadn't been left sticking in his heel.

~

Marin straightened her desktop and stood up to receive her guests. A framed navigational chart of Cape Hatteras hanging on the wall seemed to distract Wade, but Anna Lisa walked into the office like she owned the place. The lone employee, she was grateful for the company. Plus, she couldn't help but notice a deepening level of comfort between the two.

"Note to self—you need better artwork in here," Anna Lisa quipped as she arranged the guest chairs to her liking. She followed the comment with a generous look like she had something specific in mind.

"I take what's donated," Marin replied. "Eli Etheridge gave me that for the office the night he was voted onto our board of directors."

Wade turned his head and approached the desk. "Eli was a friend of my father's. Those two shared a few adventures out on the open sound. I think he taught my dad how to duck hunt. Why anyone would go out on the water in the bitterest cold under stormy skies, I'll never know. Give me a fishing pole on Cape Point any day."

"I saw a few of those poles in the cart shed," Marin added, "right beside your collection of channel buoys."

He winced at the mention as he settled into a chair beside Anna Lisa. "Oh. That came off as part of my eclectic open-water phase." He dipped his brow at Anna Lisa. "I ought to check out the poles, though. I'm sure Tyde kept them up for me."

Marin handed Anna Lisa the application for the state grant. "Speaking of Tyde, could we dream a little on his behalf? Before we look at the land use plan and how to interface public facilities with private retreats, maybe we could find a way to include what Tyde really wants, a sound-side recreation concession."

Wade appeared stunned as the paper seemed to become too hot for Anna Lisa to touch, so he took possession.

"He gave up that dream when the bank said 'no' to the loan," she replied, her tone flat.

"What kind of recreation concession?"

"Small row boats like Water Strider, sunfish sailboats, stand up paddleboards—all passive use, nothing motorized," Marin clarified. "He wants to do half-day and full-day rentals, just like the hang gliding kites on Jockey's Ridge. Tyde thinks Roanoke Sound is the next natural tourist venue for the Outer Banks. He wants to open the door and usher it in."

"But this application is for a grant, not a loan," Wade replied.

"All the more reason to apply, don't you think?

Some savvy North Carolina businessman is going to become the proud recipient and I don't see why it couldn't be Tyde. The subsequent loan portion is optional, if he wanted to expand inventory in the future."

"He'd have to be guaranteed waterfront to make this concept work." Wade slid the paper onto the edge of the desk and fished a pair of reading glasses out of his shirt pocket. "Excuse my old man move," he teased with a wink.

"Even though the Fearing exclusion clause claims no less than twenty percent of the tract's total acreage, I've drafted a plan that left your family a third of the shoreline. That initially arose from a sense of fairness on my part, but I feel it's defendable, given the family's history of deriving its livelihood from the waters of the sound."

Wade shifted forward in the chair. "What does that come to in linear feet?"

"My estimate comes in around twenty-five to thirty feet," she replied. "That's about what Tyde uses now."

"That's plenty of room to work if you're talking small boats. What about boat storage or a dock? We'd have to determine components for phase one under the grant."

"Well, I looked into putting in a floating dock. The regulatory permit process alone takes four to six months. The Rec Department doesn't have the money for a dock on their portion, so we'd likely be looking at that as a future improvement for the concessionaire."

A knowing grin surfaced on Wade's face. "Unless we had an application already grandfathered in place. Another young Fearing had a similar dream some time ago, and his father filed the application and obtained the permit for a permanent dock. We just never built it."

Anna Lisa's shocked look certainly didn't top her own. An electric charge started in her toes and traveled up through her middle, making breathing a struggle. "Something tells me they'd have to let us build, if it's already been permitted. You know, this could be our real ace-in-the-hole to make the whole plan work."

Anna Lisa uncrossed her legs and leaned in. "It would just mean the world to Tyde."

"Especially when we reveal it to him the day of the grand opening dedication," Marin stated with a wink. "I know it's a big risk trying to get it right without Tyde's input. That's why I'm posing it to you guys today, to solicit your support."

"Count me in," Wade said. "As a matter of fact, let me take the lead on this grant."

"By all means, Wade. I have my hands plenty full with the remainder of the plan."

"I think this business venture speaks volumes about how much my son means to you," he replied. Anna Lisa slid her hand over his and they intertwined fingers.

A load shifted off her shoulders. Marin stood feeling lighter than air. She now had the help she needed to pull off the whole concept.

"And maybe it will help take away the sting of losing the Fearing cottage," Anna Lisa said as she stood to join her.

Wade snagged the application as he rose. "Now I'm more than anxious to see that land use plan."

She gestured toward the conference room knowing this first round of disclosure would be the most difficult, as it represented the most intense personal scrutiny—from the existing landowners. As they centered themselves in front of the aerial photograph, she allowed Wade to take the command chair.

He touched its surface and traced the shrub line with his fingers, ending up at the Fearing cottage. The vellum curled into place next and the dream park unfurled with all its draft components. Anna Lisa made a tiny gasp as Wade's fingers traced the proposed features from the parking lot down the winding trail to the cart shed.

"Wade, your arrival the other night inspired that wandering approach," Marin said. "I combined two elements—a meandering nature trail and the primary approach to our historic feature. Though we can't move the shed, we can certainly plan around it to our heart's content."

"Then let's call the trail 'Wade's Wander' and have it mean something to the family," Anna Lisa replied. Her arm reached across his shoulders to bridge the gap between them.

He leaned into the gesture and kissed her cheek. Refocused, his fingers traced the small cart shed outline and then slid to overshadow the cottage's present location. "Hard to believe the main house will be gone." His hollow tone held an inconceivable loss.

Marin stood firm in her resolve for the project. "Which is why the rest of this plan has to be done right, to make it worth the cost." And as chief spokesperson, she'd really have to sell it.

Chapter 18

Tyde elbowed through the swinging kitchen doors, dumped two picked over salads into the trash can, and glanced at the grill. Next, he popped the faucet on and drenched his hands.

Marin arranged two bread knots on a plate on the front counter. "Don't forget your parents are coming in tonight for a romantic dinner."

"Guess what? Lonnie Grayton is here with that slender lady from the Chamber of Commerce." He spattered the whole sink area, grabbed more paper towels than needed, and dried his hands.

"Funny he should chase down the chick in the pencil skirt. She probably couldn't run away fast enough." Marin lined up the other plate with bread and added butter slabs, then balanced them on a tray. Like clockwork, Maisie appeared and took the order from her. Free for the moment, she wrapped her arms around his waist as he stood beside the grill.

Indulging in a quick kiss, he turned and swept the skewers off the direct flames. "I need two scoops of coleslaw with these, please. Did I tell you? Something's up with Bushwhack. Joey Tate stopped by earlier while I was cleaning the boat out."

"Maybe it's a good thing Lonnie is otherwise distracted right now."

"Maybe so." He pulled the skewers off the grill at the perfect time.

She slid a plate under them, each bearing a mound of coleslaw. Two generous ladles of rice later they found their way to a tray.

"Ooh, I like the looks of that," a woman's voice commented.

He turned to find his parents being brought through the kitchen toward the back screened-in porch by ever-efficient Maisie.

Marin rummaged through a drawer and found a lighter, then led them to their special seating. Wade saluted and disappeared into darkness with the parade.

Within seconds, someone clapped in approval, so Tyde knew the candles had been lit. Taking skewers from the soaking bin, he loaded four more mixed grill specials and selected the biggest shrimp in the cooler.

"Dinner salads with two mixed grills," Maisie ordered as she passed back through.

Marin appeared next, bearing a sheepish grin on her face. She opened the refrigerator and pulled out a dessert tray containing dainty lemon curd tarts. Shaking a can of whipped topping vigorously, she dotted each one with a crown. The treats returned to cold storage with a slam of the door.

Tyde soon encountered a finger dripping with the non-dairy topping. He popped it in his mouth and savored the sweet result. Marin made a purring sound and disappeared into the front, leaving him licking his lips for more. When the doors squeaked open again, Jeremy shot into the kitchen, a not-so-delicious replacement.

He stashed tub a half full of dirty plates by the dishwasher. "Hey, that blond surfer dude is asking for you. What should I tell him?"

Tyde positioned the loaded skewers across the grill bars and wiped his hands on a damp towel hanging on the oven door. "Trade me for two minutes of kitchen duty and let me go out there. It could be a matter of life or death."

Jeremy's eyes bugged out as he splashed the faucet on to wash up.

"Take two side salads to the back porch for me. And stay out of those lemon tarts, they're counted." He shoved his way out into the dimly lit dining area and navigated to Lonnie's table. Drinks had been replenished and their plates sat empty, so he couldn't see what the issue was.

"Tyde, I wanted you to meet Gwyneth," Lonnie said, his tone lacking the usual casualness. "Do you remember her from the day of your announcement about the shed?"

"Yeah, I think you were with the Chamber of Commerce delegation, weren't you? I suffered from a little stage fright that day, so I might not be remembering exactly right."

"No—you're right," she answered in a musical tone, her face animated.

He glanced over at Lonnie and could see his friend was enthralled.

"I met Lonnie that day at your place and he offered

to give me the nickel tour of some little known attractions you locals are hiding from the rest of us."

Tyde shook his head with a sly smile. "Ah yes, the old nickel tour. And something tells me you're now in-the-know, but fell haplessly for the tour guide nonetheless."

Lonnie gave her a catty wink.

Gwyneth dabbed her mouth with her napkin and blushed. "Okay—the outcome wasn't that predictable, but something along those lines."

Her cloying perfume attempted to give him a headache, so he shifted over to slap Lonnie's shoulder. "Your brother Kyle came in last week with his lady friend. I sure appreciated his help when Jimbo went down."

"How's the big guy coming along?"

"He's home now. We hope to have him back for Independence weekend. It's going to be hectic around here otherwise."

Lonnie's date perked up at the mention of the holiday, so Tyde braced for her incidental comment. "I'm on the fireworks committee and we're spending a fortune for the display this year. Plan on coming on out to the Nags Head Pier and enjoy the show with us, Tyde."

Inviting as it may have seemed to her, he wasn't too ready to return to the pier with Lonnie. "I think Marin said something about watching the Manteo display over the sound, but I'll sure mention it to her. Gotta get back to the grill. I'm probably burning my parents' dinner."

An incredulous look crossed Lonnie's face. "Was that your dad I saw walk through?"

Tyde paused at the swinging door and let the

satisfaction ripple through him. How many times had he wanted to say it? And now he finally had his chance. "Yeah, Dad's back on the Outer Banks." He had to admit, it had a good ring to it.

~

Business crept toward closing time, but Marin had considerable more cleanups to do. Tyde assisted Jeremy with bussing the last few tables out front while Maisie counted leftover desserts. She had taken a plate of four lemon curd tarts into the back porch over twenty minutes ago. The patrons there seemed unusually subdued. Maybe they had spent too much time apart to be rushed at this point. They deserved to be the last ones out, despite having displaced her at mealtime. She and Tyde had sat on the tailgate of his Jeep and enjoyed every mouthful together.

With the last of the plates loaded in the dishwasher, she straightened in time to see the diners reappear from the back porch. Anna Lisa had an interesting look on her face as Wade slipped his hand back for hers. Marin pressed an empty serving tray against her ribs and thought she recognized the shared look.

Wade halted near the doorway. "Can you get Tyde to come back?"

"Sure thing." Marin darted through the swinging doors. Maisie exited right behind her and she could hear her giggle. Tyde stood at the drink dispenser, replacing a stack of clean glasses for tomorrow's crowd.

"You're parents are asking for you in the back." She made a little face at him that made him smile back as he turned toward the kitchen. "Mind if I tag along?"

Instead of answering, he caught her up in his arms and used her as a shield.

As she parted the doors for him, she laughed and tried to gain separation to look presentable.

He grabbed her arm and pulled her back to his side. Something moved in her peripheral vision and she saw her kid sister and Jeremy peeking over the doors.

Wade nodded toward the glowing artist on his arm. "We have something to announce."

Anna Lisa looked at Tyde and let her gaze drop to Marin. "Wade has asked me to renew our vows as husband and wife."

Marin heard Maisie giggle through the louvers on the door panel and noticed Jeremy's feet move closer to hers. The air seemed electric with attraction.

Tyde held his arms out toward them. "Well, what's your answer, for heaven's sakes?"

Wade ran his fingers through his hair the same way Marin had seen Tyde do a hundred times. If she hadn't been holding his right hand, he probably would have copied his father in mirror image.

Anna Lisa brought her hands up under her chin. "I told him I'd be most honored to. Nothing would give me greater pleasure than to be his wife again." Her eyes misted at the admission and her bottom lip trembled ever the slightest bit.

Marin heard Maisie's half-giggle which stopped like something had cut it short. A glance at the doorway revealed Jeremy's white-knuckled grip on the panels, holding it closed. Before she could inspect further, Tyde wrapped her up in a bear hug of mammoth proportion as Wade embraced Anna Lisa. A kiss followed and, while she collected herself, Maisie popped into the kitchen and made a beeline for the refrigerator. Pulling out what remained of the lemon tarts, she disappeared back into the dining room, a couple of folded bills riding high in her back pocket. Worse yet, her notice-me pink lip gloss had been smeared down her chin. Love had just pulled a perfect trifecta, right in Jimbo's restaurant, a fairly heady feat in her estimation.

"We'd like to offer to pitch in with the cleanup tonight, so Marin could go home," Wade said. "I'm no good with the service up front, but I sure know how to pull KP duty back here. How does that sound?"

The apron Marin wore came untied like Cinderella's and she twirled to add effect, blowing a good-bye kiss in Tyde's direction.

He disappeared into the dining room as she washed her hands free of dinner fare for thirty-five paying patrons. He came back with Maisie trapped on his hip in forced departure. Clutching an empty tray, the girl smiled like she was on a high, oblivious to anything else in the room. Wade commandeered the tray as Tyde scooped her into his empty arm and escorted them both to the side door.

He kicked the screen door open. "Fare-thee-well, Evans girls." He released Maisie and managed to pat her head before she stepped out of range.

Marin faced around for a final tease, hoping to make him blush for a change. "Are you sure you didn't let the cute one get away?" She batted her eyelashes to help him consider his answer.

A pot clunked in the sink behind them as he lifted her even closer. His eyes made inventory of her features before he spoke. "Never mistake girl-cute with woman-beautiful," he whispered, his gaze caressing her face. The last thing she remembered was the feel of his cheek against hers, sliding ever closer to the goodnight kiss she longed for in the still of the night. It came with tender abandon, a real lesson in fortitude and patience. Too bad it had to end in the glare of headlights with her sister's mocking laugh riding the sea breeze.

~

Tyde set the full dishwasher in motion. "Hey, good tactical move on the re-hitching."

His father faced him from the sink and fed him a wry smile. "Thanks, son. Hope you can stand to have me around while. Don't know exactly where I'll hang my hat a majority of the time, but we hope to have a little getaway here on the sound, at least until your mother retires her paintbrush."

After nodding, Tyde swept around the kitchen collecting wet towels and stained pot holders. He stuffed them into a plastic bag tied onto the handle of the side door while his thoughts lingered on the getaway remark. "Did you get a chance to give Marin some meaningful input on the exclusion parcel?"

"I think so. She's being generous with the shoreline allotment in our favor, so I'm interested to see if that gesture survives general scrutiny at the public hearing."

"What about the rest? If you and mom want a getaway, we'd better have enough width on the exclusion, or somebody loses sight of the waterline."

"Yeah, I asked Marin to reshape that. If we pull away from the cart shed in back, it would give us an adequate diameter for two cottages to cozy up side-by-side."

He knotted the trash bag and hoisted it from the receptacle. "So what did that look like?"

His father cleared his throat. "Well, it went from

resembling a squatty rectangle to something akin to a dumpy spin-top. Marin named it the 'Fearing channel buoy' out of spite." Crimson appeared above his shirt collar as his expression turned sour.

A laugh escaped that spilled into the rendering and Tyde couldn't stop it to save his life.

"She's flat-out nailed you, Dad." He kicked the screen door open, headed for the dumpster.

"Don't I know it? My reputation precedes me in what I've left behind," Wade replied. "That shed cleanout is going to be a nightmare…"

Tyde pitched the day's trash into the metal bin and wondered what made hoarders fail to let go.

~

Marin plopped down in her spot at the kitchen table. "My feet are so hot, I think the gel heel in my walking shoes just melted." In two seconds, she had the shoes off, wringing her feet back into consciousness.

"Here's the mail," Maisie replied. A handful of envelopes and flyers hit the table offering a nice distraction.

A realtor's name on a glossy pamphlet caught her eye and she inhaled. "Here's the auction flyer that's going to change my life." She tore open the seal.

Maisie brought the milk jug back with her and read over her shoulder. "Absolute auction. August 25th at six o'clock on site."

"That's so all the bidders can take a closer look at what they're getting. We'll have to get this cottage showplace perfect that day. I plan to outbid them all and win ultimate possession."

"Then I hope you're saving all your tip money," Maisie replied as she snatched the flyer for a closer look.

Marin massaged her right foot and fear pulse through her at the thought of competition. If the auction was well-attended, the going ante could escalate in a heartbeat and soar right out of her range early on, a disparaging outcome.

Maisie snapped the flyer at her. "What does this mean? 'Structure only. Must be relocated off estate within thirty days of auction date.'"

Marin froze like someone was playing a practical joke. "Where are you reading that?" Her voice drained of positive emotion. When Maisie pointed a purple fingertip at an asterisk by the word "gatehouse," her line of sight trailed down to the fine print at the bottom. Nearly illegible, the caveat stung her eyes like vinegar. "From the way it sounds, they're just getting rid of the cottage—like it's in their way or something." Marin dropped her head as tears threatened.

"Not in their way, maybe simply not needed on the estate anymore." Maisie took a swig directly out of the jug and replaced the cap. "God could be telling you to nestle in somewhere else, which is the opposite of what he's telling Tyde. Funny timing, isn't it?" The teen stashed the jug and started to leave the room.

"Hilariously funny, right? He gets excluded and I get…evacuated."

Maisie turned back, her brow wrinkled. "You mean evicted, unless you win the auction."

"Now I have to win, don't I?" Marin slammed her palms down as the flyer glared back at her in a taunt. This was her little home, and she was determined to fight for it.

Chapter 19

Tyde examined the scale-down of Marin's land use plan she'd delivered to the restaurant, finally having time to look at it back home. The night grew late and Marin seemed fixed on staring at the sound in hopes of seeing Maisie return in Water Strider with Jeremy. A midnight float has seemed innocent enough when they'd first posed it.

The screen door popped open and she came back in, her face pulled tight with emotion. Any suggestions tweaking the plan could wait, as she clearly couldn't bear something much longer."Come sit with me," he said with sweet sincerity as he patted the chair beside him. "They'll be all right out there."

She folded her arms but came anyway, which sent mixed signals. "A storm's coming up from the west." She propped her elbows on the table and planted her face in her palms.

There was a storm brewing, but it wasn't out on the western horizon and Tyde knew it. He leaned over, kissed her hair, and kneaded her shoulder with his fingertips. His mother laughed from the hammock on the porch. "Know what? You're blowing me away with this park plan, Marin. I want more time to study it. The way everything is fitted onto the lot, well, I don't know how you did it. You kept the natural stuff and made improvements to the bare sand."

"Thanks, Tyde," she replied, her words partly muted by her hands. They sounded gooey, like they were sticking together in her mouth.

He nibbled at her knuckle trying to break inside her fortress, but it didn't seem to work. "Let's talk about this later so you don't have to live it twenty-four seven. Want to kick the lovebirds out of the hammock and assume custody?" A long pause passed and he thought he saw her ribcage begin to tremble.

"Birds have nests and foxes have holes, but I may not have anywhere to lay my head," she quoted.

The hurt look she gave him landed like a brick. He hunkered down to her level so he could stare right into her eyes. Maybe a meaningful translation would render itself through their gaze. Otherwise God would have to impart him with the Wisdom of Solomon, because he didn't get her allusion, not an inch of it. "But you have a place to live. I'm the soon-to-be transient." He nibbled at her jaw this time with the hope humor could melt her reticence.

"The auction flyer for my gatehouse came in the mail yesterday. In the fine print, it mentioned a real zinger. The cottage has to be relocated off the property within thirty days of the sale. I thought I was buying a home on the sound, not a timberwork box on wheels. Now I don't know what to do. Should I go look for land? Will I even have any money left after the auction to pay for it? How do you move a house anyway? It's too much for me. I can't do this." Frustration broke her confession into sobs as she fell to pieces.

He took her hands in his and tugged her closer. "One thing at a time, that's how you tackle a challenge like this. If you truly love that little place and want to keep living in it, make your very best attempt with the auction bidding. When that 'sold' call goes up, the compass will point in a new direction and you'll be in a position to strategize the next portion of the plan." When she dropped her forehead onto his shoulder with a moan, he wrapped her in a bear hug to squeeze out the hurt. Thunder rumbled from the porch and his father made an indistinguishable comment.

"Why couldn't I just keep living on the sound's edge where I am?" she lamented. "Manteo is such a cute little town and it feels so Mayberry-perfect living there on the Andy Griffith estate. Maybe that's all been part of my ongoing delusion, and God is trying to show me some reality."

He opened his mouth to respond but a flash of lightning illuminated the doorway, followed by a quick report of thunder. When his father appeared outside the screen door, he jerked his head up from their intimate conversation.

"Let's get those teenagers back in," Wade said as he glanced out over the sound. "Storm's getting closer. Do you have another boat?"

"Just Grandpa's racing scull up in the rafters—and your long board under the stairs." Tyde rose from the table. Marin tensed as she stood beside him. The air smelled like electricity.

Wade motioned him out. "Long board then, if we

have to go out, that is."

Tyde brushed a kiss on her cheek and hit the door with his palm. Within seconds, another flash split the night and he could trace the outline of an anvil-shaped thunderhead as it moved up from Manteo. Under it, the sound waters turned midnight blue.

His mother hurried into the house. "Take a flashlight, Tyde."

His feet found the deck shoes on the second step, now dry and crusty from his crab run earlier. Marin pressed up against his back and he turned to offer her a reassuring hug. Sounds of scraping sand hastened his efforts and he parted with a kiss on her lips. A flashlight struck his shoulder and he grabbed it for the rescue. By the time he had descended the stairs, the skeg end of the long board appeared, dragging through the sand. He gathered it to his hip and brushed the sand off an ancient wax job.

Wade led the way to the water in silent strength.

"Remember how to do this, Dad?" He craned his neck to size up the storm as his feet rehearsed the distance between stepping-stones in the dark.

"Cake walk on a long plank," Wade replied. "Tell them to stay near the phone. I've got my cell."

The porch light diminished with each step toward the sound, and when he turned around, the women were huddled into a solitary silhouette by the railing. "Stay by the phone and we'll call," he yelled. "Do *not* come out in the storm."

"Good point," Wade added. "The last thing we need is two more storm victims."

"Better safe than sorry." Tyde angled behind him as they crossed Soundside Road. He searched the waterline for the running lights on top of Water Strider's bait box, as he had insisted that Jeremy run legal with them on the bow.

Wade exhaled as he approached the water's edge. "Those kids could be anywhere. Try calling them out before we launch and get wet."

Tyde lowered the board to the sand. "Maisie? Jeremy?" he called through cupped hands. Only the storm answered, and it didn't sound too happy.

Wade stooped to place the surfboard on the water's surface. "Front or back, Tyde?"

He squinted into the inky black and studied the channel markers for a position. "Let me be the eyes tonight." He waded into the water to take his position. "You provide the power stroke, okay? We'll switch on the way back in." After stripping off his T-shirt, he knelt on the nose of the board. With a forceful shove, they were off.

~

Marin peeked at the skillet-shaped clock on the kitchen wall and it read seven minutes past her last check. Anna Lisa had left the wraparound porch without a word but reappeared with a painting in her hands. She held it up for her inspection and the porch became a scene-within-a-scene. This time the profile of Tyde had been painted in except for traces of white canvas around his eyes. Something ethereal about the artwork lent her peace, which lasted until the next rumble of thunder shook the planks underfoot. "Why does this painting do something to my mindset?"

Anna Lisa gave a little chuckle and began to walk back to her room to put it away. "Could it be because you're in love with the waterman in the picture? And maybe it strikes you that he's fixed on the distant horizon because it outlines the sound with an aqueous lure."

It came like a jolt, the realization that she was being petty and self-centered about the gatehouse auction. The man she loved was set to lose so much more—the familiar perch from which he viewed the entire world. "If I have any money left after the house auction, I'd like to buy that painting," she replied as she followed Anna Lisa part way around the porch toward the bedroom wing.

"Sorry, it's not for sale." The artist shrugged and disappeared into her room.

In the quiet that followed, Marin did the mental math to tally her total savings. The number from her latest bank statement didn't include her jar of accumulated tip money or the Associated Press check for the article. JD would beef that up with what he owed her and it still wouldn't give her the financial boost she needed if the auction skyrocketed. She began a vocal exhalation, but a close lightning strike put a quick end to her complaint. Percussion from the strike boomed across the night.

Anna Lisa returned to the porch. "That one gave me goose bumps." She began to release the hammock from its anchor pin on the house. "Let's keep this from getting wet. Can you help me?"

"Sure thing." Marin shifted toward the post along the railing that held the far end of the hammock. "Please forgive me for being moody tonight. I found out some tough news about the upcoming auction for my gatehouse that's had me a little preoccupied. I should be more concerned for two teenagers right now anyway."

"What about the auction? You were expecting it, weren't you?" She began to roll the braided ropes of the hammock up.

Marin held tension on the far end. "Yes, I was expecting it. But a stipulation added in small print details that the house has to be moved off the premises. That pulled the rug out from under my feet. It appears the auction doesn't involve any real estate under said dream house, so the sound-side land becomes like batteries for a toy, not included in the boxed deal."

Anna Lisa pulled on her end of the hammock. "Drat and double drat." With the swing in tow, they clopped down the stairs in tandem and dropped the rope contraption into a gear box beneath the porch.

Marin could barely see what she was doing. "Guess I'll close up the cart shed." Within steps, she encountered her first raindrop of the night. That hastened her gait and she sighed in relief when the ancient wood didn't pose any objections. She liked her historic features nice and compliant. It added to their present-day charm.

Anna Lisa pulled in a faded flag while she returned to the porch. As soon as she made the top of the stairs, she checked the time. It was twelve-forty. Now she could begin to worry. The night air smelled heavy with ozone and within seconds, a curtain of rain poured all around the porch. The air chilled and passed a shiver across her bare shoulders.

Anna Lisa motioned her in. "Time to move the party inside." A blue flash played on her concerned face.

Marin took her hand as she passed through the

doorway. "Let's pray for the rescuers."

"And the boating teenagers," Anna Lisa added with a motherly smile. Thunder roared against their hope and the smile disappeared before she could close her eyes. "Lord, help the men find the kids and get them safe out of this storm tonight, in Jesus name, amen."

A triple strike followed the prayer and the thunder claps overlaid each other like a pack of barking Rottweiler dogs. Marin took comfort from a tender touch and squeezed the artist's hand as she extended her friendship into the gut-wrench of the storm's arrival. A piece of the sky tore off in electric blue laser and the atmosphere objected right away.

~

Tyde tried to wipe his eyes clear, but it only brought more water. Something moved against the black. "There—at eleven o'clock—a bobbing light." He spat rain as he formed the words.

"Stand up and wave the flashlight," Wade replied. "I've got the board."

Tyde attempted to stand despite his quaking knees. He spread his feet until he found some gritty wax to resist his motion and lend traction. "Jeremy?" He beamed the light out toward the faint light combo. Seconds ticked by until the bait box lights did a complete one-eighty turn. "Yes! They see us."

"Great job, son, now let them come to us as we're shoreward. He's likely been disoriented by the storm."

"*You* come to *us*," he shouted into the rain. Small and helpless, all he could think to do was turn the flashlight into a beacon and let it pulse out a return path. When the bait box lights made another correction, he dropped to his knees in relief.

Wade muscled up behind him to a crouch and worked the cell phone out of his pocket. "Let's spread some good news to the women back on the porch."

In the rimming light of the beacon, Tyde could see relief etched on his face.

Wade punched buttons through a waterproof cover as the sky went blue with anger. A sound tantrum followed, so he held up until the sky had its say. "We found 'um. They're rowing to us now. I'll let you know when we make the shore. Have some towels ready." He lowered the phone and slid back toward the rear, sinking the board deeper in the water. "I think old faithful here has a hull leak. My end's waterlogged. Why don't you get in with the kids and row them back home?"

"Okay, but let's stay close just the same. Agreed?" A flash of lightning blinded him and he squeezed his eyes closed, waiting for the thunder. The sound waters lapped over the board.

"Agreed. You don't think you're going to be shed of me that easy, do you?" Wade laughed.

A small knife twisted in his side, which Tyde attributed to exhaustion, not abandonment.

"Not too afraid of that. How were the women holding up?"

"Let's just say the sky isn't the only thing crying. Get ready to grab that gunwale."

In seconds the bow of Water Strider floated into his hands with two drowned rats at the oars. When he boarded the craft, he almost knocked them overboard in his exuberance.

"You guys trade me the stern for the bow." He lent Maisie a steady hand to aid the transition.

Wade turned the long board and paddled for home. "After you, captain," he said. Maisie reached out a trembling arm and touched the stalwart paddler as the boat inched passed him. With a solitary oar stroke, they surged back to the safety of shore.

~

Marin inhaled the hot cocoa Anna Lisa had simmering on the stove top and glanced through the screen door, expectant to see some signs of the search party. Her sinuses hurt from the drop in barometric pressure—and all the crying—but it seemed like a small price to pay for the cleansing she now felt inside. In passing, she skimmed her palm over the top towel as she pushed the screen door open enough to see the shore below. No signs of life yet.

Her hostess stirred the pot. "Consider this. I'd like to have your back at the gatehouse auction. If the bid runs past your savings, my money could serve as a buffer. You decide how much based on your comfort level."

Too astonished for words, Marin's mouth hung open until a high-pitched sound pricked her ear. "That's my sister," she exclaimed while rushing to the porch. She grabbed an umbrella, skittered down the stairs, and heard Anna Lisa trailing right behind her. The stepping-stones passed with regularity as they made their way across the road to the shore. Four drenched members of the rescue party huddled in the rain until she gave them shelter under her umbrella.

Anna Lisa held hers above Wade and melted into his arms.

In the flashlight's beam, Marin could make out her sister's expression of relief and somehow the weight of all the world's wrongs washed off her into the sand. A strong hand pulled at her and she complied to find herself at Tyde's side. With an arm around his neck, she tiptoed into a kiss that landed cold, wet, and reverberating with life. The collision left her breathless.

"Let's get to the kitchen where I have hot cocoa waiting," Anna Lisa said. Wade pulled Jeremy to his side to lend him some support.

Marin clutched Maisie. "How was that for a memorable night on the water?"

Maisie paused enough to wipe her face on her dry shirt and gave her a wobbly smile. "Beyond memorable, I'm talking epic bragging rights."

Marin pushed wet bangs out of her wide eyes. At least their feet were on land now.

Once within the porch light's glow, Tyde clicked the flashlight off and took possession of the umbrella to stabilize it in the wind. The stairs loomed up ahead. Inexplicably, the world flashed blue between them and the cottage. In the deafening explosion that followed, Maisie fell to her knees.

Wade shoved Jeremy and Anna Lisa behind him and ran up the porch steps unprotected while Tyde backed her away from the structure.

Anna Lisa followed close enough that Marin could see something angular riding atop her umbrella. She grabbed it and brought it in for closer inspection. "Roof shingle," she stammered, holding it up for Tyde to see. Her gaze trailed up to discover an odd orange glow cavorting against the pitch black of the storm. The roof ridge illuminated, a living nightmare.

Tyde lunged from their tight huddle. "Dad—fire on the roof."

Marin tried to breathe, but the downpour wouldn't allow it. Fear had come to set a spell, right on the roof of the Fearing cottage. Historic or not, it proved highly combustible despite the soaking rain. "God, please, no," she managed, but the dueling elements raced across the roof to spite her. When Maisie whimpered from the sand, her knees threatened to buckle.

Chapter 20

A panicked rage set into Tyde's bones as he entered the bedroom wing to drag out Grandpa Walt's possessions he'd packed earlier into two storage tubs. Back on the porch seconds later, he glanced up to see help waiting in the wings—and he sure needed it.

He beckoned the teen closer with urgency. "Jeremy, take these clear of the house." His mother appeared with drawers pulled from the kitchen cabinets, closely followed by Marin and Maisie. Jeremy approached and yanked the tubs off the porch.

Wade dashed from the bedroom with duffle bags packed under both arms and Anna Lisa's art easel gripped in his hand. "Load the cars," Wade said, assessing the downpour in a glance. "I called the fire department. Tyde, go get your stuff next. I'll work on the rest."

As he paused to wipe his face on a towel, Tyde gauged the danger of going back inside by the depth of wrinkles on his father's face. They regarded one another.

Wade shook his head. "We'll have to decide whether to let the house burn down—or try to save it."

Headed for his room, the realization that this could be the end gagged him. He rummaged through his dresser and slung handfuls of clothes into a canvas bag until it became too full to close. When he scanned the room for valuable treasures, he discovered that most of it was trinkets and trash, the faded posters of teenage whims. He grabbed a sailboat carved from ebony wood and laid it atop the clothes. A clatter of framed photos joined them and he hurried from the room with the load, afraid to look back.

Taking the stairs three at a time, he made it to his mother's SUV when the first fire truck rumbled up the road. He stashed the bag in her floorboard and ran toward the road to flag down the rescuers. The rain let up and he stole a glance at the cottage. Its high-pitched roof gaped open and hell's inferno poured out the top like a volcanic vent. The truck's headlights blinked and he motioned them deeper into the yard. A police car with lights and sirens blazing lurched in behind the truck, so Tyde ran back to meet the crew. "Lightning strike," he said as he struggled to breathe. The smoke descended in a haze around them. Before he knew it, Joey Tate stood beside him, regret written all over his face. "Jeremy's safe. He's helping the women clear the kitchen."

Joey fisted the radio. "Anybody hurt? I'll call in the ambulance?"

Tyde stepped over to the SUV and opened a door for Jeremy and Maisie as they deposited another load. "No one's hurt, Joey, thank God. These two were out on the sound for a midnight cruise when the storm hit. Had it not been for us out rescuing them, we all could have been in the house. But we were right out here, just coming up the path when the lightning bolt struck the roof."

Joey nodded as a smaller fire truck arrived, rushing into the yard. The fire crew began to circle the house in assessment. "Everyone away from the house," an amplified voice called. In a light sprinkle, the teens tripped down the front stairs carrying what they could.

Tyde met them at the car and helped stash the belongings inside.

Wade retreated to drag the carcass of an old sailboat from under the cottage. Anna Lisa trailed off to help him as the rest gave up and pulled back.

Now the words he needed to say wouldn't come, as Joey led him toward the returning firemen.

"We can get a hose up..." the crew chief began.

Tyde halted him with a flattened palm. Wade joined them and nodded, lending him the confidence he needed in the moment. "The house is scheduled for demolition next month. Can we just let it burn? No neighbors are close by."

The chief's jaw dropped at the mere suggestion. Suppression was their modus operandi, and he didn't seem to like departing from it.

Marin ran up and pointed off the far porch railing. "The cart shed—you've got to protect the cart shed." Fire transferred laterally along the roof ridge and had set the library wing ablaze. Her fear-filled face reflected the widespread devastation.

It all materialized like a bad dream to Tyde. His feet turned to lead and his mind went blank. Smoke began to burn his eyes.

"It's historic and has to be saved," Wade shouted.

The chief found new vigor and a target for his suppression, his arm churning the night air signaling the truck to pull up across the sand yard. Joey stood with his hand collaring his brother's neck while the youth watched in unmasked horror. Fire sank into the hull of the bedroom wing and the crackling lick of flames spread like hunger. The rain had slacked off at last, allowing the fire to consume the night.

Tyde surveyed the group for a head count. "Hey, where's Mom?" Red lights flickered against the yellow blaze as the fire crew repositioned the truck toward the row house.

Wade ran his fingers through his wet hair. "She was right behind me five seconds ago." Part of the roof collapsed over the bedroom wing, releasing a roar of fire.

"The painting…of Tyde," Marin stammered. "She wanted to go back for it earlier, but we wouldn't let her."

When Tyde stepped toward the house, his father stiff-armed him back with a jolt. "Let me," he insisted. "No one else comes in. Got it?"

His demanding tone rang familiar and, in the moment, Tyde grew helpless and unsure of himself. Flames fully engulfed the bedroom wing as he stared at its flank. A woman screamed right about the time Wade leapt into the flames. A wet hand slipped into his, tethering him in place. His throat threatened to close.

"God, please help us get Anna Lisa back out of the house and you can let the fire have all the rest," Marin prayed.

When her lips pressed against his shoulder, he pushed out of his panic. He managed to swallow. Everything tasted of ashes and soot.

"Lord, help Mr. Wade get to her and then get out so they can be happy together for many years to come," Maisie added, a tremble in her voice. Marin pulled her closer and she tucked under Tyde's far side for a huddle.

Joey patted his shoulder and nodded to the patrol car where Jeremy stood by an open rear door. "Let's get you ladies under cover and out of harm's way," he offered.

Tyde tugged at the women in compliance. "He's right. For safety's sake, get in and take a rest."

Marin stared back with a questioning look and dragged her feet as they walked. "Tyde, with your permission, I need to take a photo of this for JD at the paper."

Allowing a public look at his inner pain seemed the last courtesy he could extend, but he read the sincerity in her face and gave her a reluctant nod.

"Nothing near the house," Joey added.

She ran off toward her car as he tucked Maisie in the back seat. Jeremy followed her in and slammed the door on the trauma out in the sand yard.

"Hope you don't mind, Tyde. I called for an ambulance when your mother went missing," Joey confessed. "Let's get as close as the heat will allow in case they call for help."

"I appreciate that Joey. Thanks for being here. I'm not thinking straight right now."

"No great wonder." He spread his arms to encompass the catastrophe. A spray of foam shot up over the cart shed as the preservation portion of the effort took shape. The outer wall of the library caved in with a crash. Distant thunder rumbled back from the ocean side.

Tyde heard the weakest sound as though the sand beneath the cottage had hatched a cough. A motion between the slats under the porch caught his attention and he broke out running before he could think. "It's my dad," he shouted back to Joey. An ambulance siren split the night as he kicked against the dry-rotted slats to reach the movement. A pair of hands appeared and he ducked in to pull his father out by the shoulders.

Wade grimaced in the fire's glow. "Easy son, Anna Lisa's hurt." With an arm locked around his wife, the man emerged out from under the cottage, his shirt partly singed off.

Tyde shoved Joey back. "Go get the ambulance closer." As the officer disappeared, agony worked up his chest. Not trusting his own hands, Tyde pulled his mother across the sand as the heat pinned them low. Incredulous as the scene unfolded in the light, she still clutched a painting under her arm.

Joey returned as the ambulance backed in. Too afraid to touch her, she lay there like an abandoned porcelain doll, scorched and missing clumps of her hair. She wouldn't open her eyes, but her arm moved.

Wade rolled on his side to face Tyde. "Take her first."

The EMT crew readily shifted to his mother as Marin dropped to his side to comfort him, her face washed with fresh tears. Unable to bear the weight of compounding trauma any longer, Tyde grabbed her where she knelt and broke apart from the inside out.

~

Marin stood beside her car, dumbfounded and weak.

Joey stepped over to her. "He'll be at my place tonight. We'll call Albemarle Hospital to get an update on his parents first thing in the morning. Are you sure you two ladies are okay?"

She placed a hand on his arm to let him know how much his help meant. "We'll be fine, just keep Tyde's chin up for me, will you Joey?"

"Bad way to come down," he muttered as he turned for the patrol car.

Maisie sobbed from the passenger side as the last fire truck pulled out of the sand yard. Nothing but a smoky haze remained except the little shed that had predated the colossal house. She had taken a closeup of the shed with its foam coating, but she paused to take one last look at the scene in her headlights. Desolation ruled the nine-acre plot, now devoid of its claim to fame.

The patrol car arced around in a three-point turn and the Dare County emblem on the door panel flashed its golden glint in her peripheral vision. Marin turned in time to see Tyde, head in hands, bent in the passenger seat. He failed to look up to say farewell, which made her feel invisible. For the first time, she feared losing him.

"Can we go now?" Maisie whined.

She dropped into the driver's seat and fumbled with the keys. The car came to life and she reached for the gear shift.

Maisie's hand rested on hers. "Sorry for the trouble we added to the night. Some storm…"

"Yeah, some storm," she repeated, weaving her fingers into her sister's. "We got you guys back in and that's what matters. I shudder to think what it would have been like if we'd been standing in the house when the lightning struck."

"You're finding the silver lining," Maisie replied, sounding sleepy. The teen wiggled and adjusted the beach towel around her waist so it covered her bare arms.

She cut the air conditioning off and lowered the windows as she backed around and exited Soundside Road. Catching a glimpse of Water Strider by the sound's edge, her thoughts crept back to Tyde. "I'm looking for God's hand in all of this, really searching him out."

"Those who seek him find him," Maisie replied with a yawn.

The remainder of the trip off the island to Manteo unfolded with quiet empathy. They would sleep with a roof over their heads for the remainder of the night while the Fearings had nothing. God would have to turn that around in one of his miraculous reversals. For her part, she would stay open to being his hands here on earth. The thought of losing Tyde resurfaced, and she shielded it from her weary mind.

~

"Hey, hey. Jimbo's back on the job," Tyde teased, his words drawn out to match the speed the restaurateur entered the kitchen.

Marin tilted her head enough he could see she was smiling. Some coleslaw took the brunt of her chopping fury as Maisie appeared with an order and disappeared like a vapor.

Jimbo shook his head and targeted a stool to park his bulk. "It's my restaurant and I don't know half the people working here." He pulled the refrigerator open and drew out the mini-dessert platter. His eyebrows arched. "Now I don't recognize the food either."

"You know what these are," Tyde replied as he lifted a steamed basket of crab from a boiling pot. He drained them with a bounce and settled them into an enamel bowl for the crab-pick-for-two.

Marin scooted two dishes of slaw down the counter and handed him the tongs to remove the veggie skewers from the grill. She filled a small plate with bread knots and rang a tiny bell hanging by the door. Jeremy appeared with the serving tray and held it level for loading.

"Jimbo, this is Jeremy, Joey Tate's kid brother and my new housemate."

"Finally, I meet the big boss," Jeremy replied, letting Marin set the food in place. "Thanks for a chance to prove myself this summer."

Jimbo harrumphed, but the kid stood his ground. "Well then, I'm glad it worked out for you," Jimbo added. "Remember to keep the customers happy out front."

Tyde looked up from the grill as the teen nodded in response. He waited for him to leave before turning to Jimbo for an update. "What can *you* eat?" he asked, holding up a shrimp skewer as bait.

A kid-wants-candy look slipped across the big man's face, but he shifted on the stool and watched Marin. "Four ounces of lean meat and all the vegetables I want. No butter, no cheese, and no condiments right now. But I'll cheat for cocktail sauce because I gotta have it."

He couldn't hold back a grin as Marin slid the owner a bowl of coleslaw and he dumped it right down his gullet.

Marin threw the warmer lid up and produced a plate. "Tyde grilled some killer swordfish steaks earlier. Would you like half of one on some rice pilaf?"

Jimbo fought with himself and then finally extended a hand for the lean portion, scrutinizing it like a food critic.

She placated him with a smile. "I prefer the mixed grill myself, but woman does not live by shrimp alone."

Maisie came in and withdrew the dessert platter. When Jimbo made grab for it, she dodged and retreated.

"That's Marin's kid sister Maisie," Tyde said. "We brought her in from Elizabeth City when we couldn't keep up with the front."

Jimbo started to reply but couldn't stop eating. He looked a little slimmer and actually had a healthy tan.

Marin wiped her brow. "I think we're heading for a lull after this order. Want to take a dinner break? Jimbo can cover if something comes up." She slid a chef salad from the fridge and went up front for their drinks.

The boss man stabbed his fork toward the back porch, giving Tyde permission to step away from the grill. "You two look cozy."

Tyde finished out the order while contemplating his response. "She's my rock. It's been rough lately. Did you hear about the cottage?"

"Yup, I heard. Nasty storm. We lost power out my way."

"Mom's still in the hospital, so Marin and I are going up tomorrow. Can you be here at five in case we run late? You'll have the kids as back-up, but they don't run the grill."

"No worries, Tyde-man. Jimbo's back in town."

Tyde snickered as Marin returned. He rang the bell and left the order. Picking his dinner from the warming tray, he grabbed her salad en route to the back porch. Despite the privacy, it didn't seem too romantic.

She attacked her salad. "The Parks Department had a hissy fit today. They want structures down on the waterfront. Wade didn't think much of having a boathouse down there as it blocks off the view for everybody."

"Including the Fearings," he replied with an emphasis on the name. "That stretch of unbroken water is part of the lure of the sound side. Better fight now to preserve it or we lose it for a lifetime. Tell you the truth, Marin, I'm done with loses."

"I'm a fairly good fighter," she replied. "And I'm not giving in an inch to that bunch. Let's see what happens at the public hearing in two weeks when we're required to take comments."

He beamed a look of appreciation her way. "I admire a woman with an invincible game plan." That land use plan represented his best chance of pulling out of his homeless existence. The in-between sure left a lot to be desired. When she leaned in toward him, he mustered enough affection to pat her cheek.

~

Though necessary, driving up separately brought lonesomeness with it that Marin didn't cherish one bit. Now Tyde had asked her to visit with Wade while he went into his mother's bedside in their shared hospital room. The tag team approach didn't appeal to her.

She found him sitting erect in the raised bed, his tanned limbs extended from a bleached hospital gown. The corner of a cotton bandage peeked out at the neckline covering his burn wounds. "Hey Wade. You look much better today."

"They're releasing me this afternoon," he replied. "Wish I had something to wear out of here. They had to cut my clothes off me in the ER."

"Tyde drove Anna Lisa's SUV up. It's in the rear lot with your duffel bag is inside. I'll go get it for you. Count on one of us driving you home. Are you going to her condo?"

"Yeah. She'll be a couple of days behind me, but I'll be there ready to take care of her when she comes home."

Touched by his devotion, she stepped closer and placed a hand on his arm."My parents want to help. My mom is already out shopping for your groceries. I'll have her meet us there when you're released. Let me get the keys from Tyde and I'll be right back." She started to ask through the curtain but the keys just appeared. Through the crack, Tyde's face swam in tears. Another storm had hit the sound.

~

The dark house hummed with refrigerator noise as Tyde shifted on the sofa, trying to make the cushion yield to his hip so he could fall sleep. Joey slammed in through the carport door and he sat up rod-straight from the clatter.

He threw his keys on the counter, regarding his guest. "Sorry man, I forgot..." He held his head in his hand. "What a rough night."

"Did you guys raid Bushwhack's place?"

Immediately sorry that he'd probed, he'd forgotten about it until now.

His host lumbered across the kitchen and pulled open the refrigerator, its light revealing a leaden face. The door closed by itself and Joey rifled through a small cabinet by the microwave. Then he came in and sat across from Tyde like he wanted to watch TV or something.

A full liquor bottle appeared on the coffee table between them. That sobered him up enough to wipe his face on the hem of his T-shirt.

"Bushwhack's dead, Tyde. He rushed the captain, so I had to shoot him. Once he was pronounced dead at the scene, I got placed on administrative leave…standard procedure and all that rot." He grabbed the bottle by the neck.

Protective, Tyde snatched it away from him. Alcohol was the last thing he needed.

Joey started to unbutton his uniform, pulled the shirttail out, and shucked it off his burly arms, throwing it in the corner. "You gonna give me that bottle back?"

"I'm going to give you some advice from the bottom of the barrel first, and then I might." He thought he heard a cuss word working its way up his friend's throat, but the sound became mixed in with the noises coming from the bathroom. They'd awakened Jeremy.

"Shoot first…and I'll ask questions later," Joey replied, his tone weary with forbearance.

The toilet flushed, so Tyde held his peace as Jeremy emerged and wandered into the living room. Thinking to hide the bottle, he lowered it to his feet.

The teen's eyes roamed from one man to the other. "Is everything okay in here?"

"Rough night," Joey repeated. "I'll tell you about it in the morning. Go get some rest."

"Solid," Jeremy replied, smoothing a hand over his bicep tattoo. "See you around noon."

A fragile silence held the hurt back as he allowed Jeremy to get back to his room. Finally the door clicked into place and he exhaled.

Joey laid his head back on the padded chair.

"Listen, if you open this bottle, then you're no better than Bushwhack. In fact, if you have to drink yourself oblivious to forget tonight's battle, then you're letting evil win in the end. Don't do it, Joey. One, it won't bring Bushwhack back, and two, what does it tell Jeremy? His big brother can't handle being on the high side of justice? Can't make peace with upholding what's right?"

The large-framed man stood and began pacing the floor. He walked a circle around the breakfast table a couple of times and finally came back to the living room."Give me the bottle."

Finding his hand, Tyde thrust it back into his possession, biting his tongue to say even one more thing. But in his chest, resolve held firm. The seal on the lid broke and he heard liquor being poured. Defeat stung his brain until he realized the liquid kept splashing for too long. The recognition soon struck— Joey was pouring it down the drain. He fell back on the sofa as his legs became noodles, the relief flooding over him more like exhaustion. Looking at life from the bottom of the barrel sure had an honest ring to it, even if it was a strain in the neck.

The empty bottle soon rattled the trash can. "Thanks for being here for me, Tyde," Joey said as he headed for his room.

He lay back down and fisted the pillow, making a dent for his head. Maybe now he could get some shut-eye before anything else burned down around him. Sleep seemed like an escape, and he needed a major dose of it.

Chapter 21

Tyde came to the public hearing because he'd promised his father he would. Otherwise, it was a waste of a perfectly good Saturday morning. He could have been clearing out the rubble from the fire, like every other day for the last two weeks. Coming through the gym door, he spotted Marin up on the platform discussing something with Eli. He needed to find a place to sit where he wouldn't cause her any trouble. Someone waved good-naturedly and he spied Hazel Aydlett summoning him forward. She sat conspicuously in the center where he didn't want to be.

He strolled up the aisle trying to think up an excuse but the elderly representative of the Historical Society stood and squeezed him so tight, his resistance vanished. The commotion hooked Marin's attention, and she gestured amicably with her clipboard as he separated himself from the well-wisher. Keeping his presence low-key had lasted all of ten seconds.

Hazel patted the arm of the seat next to hers. "I've heard your mother is home now under your father's diligent care." She settled back in like a marshmallow figure, scooting her purse to the far side to give his feet more room. The comforting smell of rosewater drifted off her skin.

Some semblance of his former self returned. "She still can't see, but the doctors believe it's only a matter of time. Dad's highly interested in this park plan, but he can't leave her yet. He had to send me as his lowly emissary. Marin knows what she's doing even if I don't."

"Don't let this adversity come between the two of you, Tyde. The man doesn't have to be the stronger partner all the time." She nodded as though she knew.

"We might just make it then," he replied. A grin tugged at his cheek and he let it go for her sake. Sparkles ignited in her gray eyes like she'd accomplished her mission. Two speakers took the stage and he straightened in his seat in time to receive a handout being distributed. Emblazoned on the glossy sheet was the Fearing park plan, with color-coded components overlaid on earth tones of natural elements. Instead of analyzing the features for any changes, he couldn't help but stare at the Fearing Exclusion. His dad's sense of humor played out like a private joke meant for him alone—the excluded tract now resembled a channel buoy. And it had a fair chunk of shoreline at its western edge. Home already had a familiar ring to it, a feeling that brought him some comfort, no matter how short-lived. When a tall man approached the podium, he shifted lower in his seat. Hazel shot him a corrective frown. Who was he hiding from?

~

Marin strained through the pandering comments of the city manager, intent to scan her notes on the proposed features in the park. Instead of allowing questions at the end of her presentation, she had designed her talk to take comments after each component, giving the public a fair chance to voice their concerns. The Dare County Advocates had been placed in charge of the public hearing, so she would have to keep it moving. She attempted a head count for their official records.

Eli stood to take the podium from the lackluster opening speaker. "This meeting might be the best SPF around for a hot July day," he quipped, adjusting the microphone stand for better results. Laughter filled the gym. "At least the air conditioning's on, even if we don't have any ice cream to serve."

"You should have," someone yelled from the back, generating another round of laughs.

Marin recognized Hazel Aydlett and her gaze froze on Tyde for a moment. Not sharing the laugh, he seemed lifeless. She picked back up on her count and stuck a finger out when she hit one hundred. The count rounded out at one hundred-eighty and she noted it on her agenda.

"An authentic act of generosity has brought us here today to announce a new public park," Eli said. "Before we delve into the various aspects of this proposal, I wanted to say a few words about how this land deal transpired. I have to warn you. It's a cliffhanger that doesn't have full resolution yet. However, as a researcher, I'm as diligent as a birddog, and I promise an end to this story on the day of our grand opening, Labor Day Monday."

Marin saw him turn a bit and the next thing she knew, he flashed a smile in her direction. She nodded to keep him moving, her gaze accidently landing where Tyde sat in the audience. She deflected the smile and tried to look composed. She only had her first sentence memorized and the rest would simply have to flow. Maybe God would give her some grace for the presentation. It had been wrought under his divine inspiration, after all.

"In my estimation we, the people of Dare County, cannot fully appreciate how the Fearings came to give us this property without understanding how they came by it in the first place. The answer harkens back to nineteen hundred and seven. Now I'm going to read from the original land title, so bear with all the 'wherefore and thereunto' lingo as the truth gets hinted at. This is section six point two point two and it reads like this…"

Eli cleared his throat which seemed to launch Marin into another dimension, one where young couples walked tranquilly along the shore without a worry in the world. The scenario birthed a longing deep within her heart, and she found the inner fortitude to claim her devotion to Tyde's land. Tense, she wrapped her fingers around her wrist to take her pulse. The watch tried to distract her with its sweeping second hand, so she turned the face where she couldn't see it. *Lead me forward, God.* When Eli mentioned the governor's name, she recognized the end of the reading approached.

"My early research indicates that this land grant reflects something of a friendly collusion between these two men, the governor and a native banks resident. I hope to garner more information to present at the grand opening, but let me hint at this. A charter of the Little Kinnakeet Lifesaving Station from eighteen ninety-nine lists the names of six seasonal employees along with the year-round keeper. And topping that list is future governor Benjamin G. Pritchard, a scant young soul nineteen years of age. The next name listed is Willis J. Fearing." The audience murmured at the revelation.

Marin looked out to see how Tyde handled the news. The effect was like someone had jolted him with a defibrillator. Signs of life surged from him as Hazel clasped her hands to her ample chest to quell her excitement.

"Another link to Little Kinnakeet still sits right on the Fearing property, a cart shed which will stand at the heart of our historic preservation portion of the park plan today. I personally feel like that little shack is trying to tell me its secret, and when it comes to history, I'm not particularly hard of hearing. Give me the remainder of this summer to ferret out what Paul Harvey used to call 'the rest of the story.'" Several people clapped at his quest for truth, including Hazel. Cordelia charged in late and sat on the end of their row looking flustered.

"Back to today, all mysteries aside. The Fearing family has been generous to the people of Dare County in offering seven acres of land for a public park. The exclusion I just read requires that the family retain no less than twenty percent, which will appear on our maps along the southern park boundary with the label 'Fearing Exclusion.' Now I understand that we have a representative of the family with us today, Tyde Fearing. I'd like to ask him to stand at this time so we can extend to him a small gesture of our appreciation."

Marin held her breath hoping he would take it upon himself to humor Eli and represent the family. To her amazement, Tyde readily stood and waved his acknowledgment to the audience first, then to Eli, as the gym filled with applause. Several men broke from their seats and came to shake his hand. He wore his blue polo shirt, the one she thought made him look like part of the sound. Affection for him rose in her veins and she couldn't stop the sensation, even after he sat down. Up next, she'd just have to take the podium under the influence of love.

~

Tyde tensed as yet another question surfaced regarding use of the waterfront. Marin had walked them through every other aspect of the plan with grace and equanimity, but the Rec Department representative had lit the fire of controversy by admitting they wanted more structural development in the future, though it lacked funding for capital improvements right now. A local seafood distributor had countered with a comment that the waterfront should be left open as a gift to generations to come. Tyde could have kissed his scaly old cheek.

When he saw Darien Grayton step up to the microphone, a dull stitch caught in his side. Good thing his father wasn't here or the two men might have resolved their differences once and for all. A glance up to the podium told him Marin didn't appreciate the gadfly's presence either.

"Darien Grayton speaking. Even though it's nice that the Fearings have given us the property for a park, I don't see why we have to tip-toe around using it like we want. There ain't enough non-motorized boat traffic for the sound side to make best use of that ramp. I've got two jet skis and would appreciate not having to put in at Wanchese every time I go out. I say open the ramp up to all users. That's my two cents."

His ingratitude for Marin's passive use of the public boat ramp didn't sit well with Tyde. He hadn't realized his fists were clenched until Hazel patted him to remain calm. The next man up asked for a fish cleaning station, which seemed reasonable. Focused on Marin, he didn't see the next speaker in line until he heard a familiar voice.

"I'm Lonnie Grayton and my comment is that I hope we can look to the future as we plan this park. I say start small and keep the ramp use light, non-motorized, and tranquil. And keep the boathouse off the shoreline to protect the open vista like planned. Someday I hope my children can play on that climber and marvel at the cart shed's place in history. I want to thank Tyde and Dare County Advocates for a breath of fresh air in how we use our resources." Leaving the microphone, he circled back around the front, nodding to Marin as he came through.

Exhilarated, Tyde rose and stepped out to meet him in the aisle for a handshake. When Lonnie slapped his back, the moment held healing, like he had his old friend back. They stood together as the next person in line began to speak. Lonnie kept his hand on his shoulder and winked.

"I'm Gwyneth Pendleton of the Dare County Chamber of Commerce. I'm here today to announce that the chamber, in its excitement over this new facility, will donate part of its budget back to the county to fund the children's fort portion of the park. In addition, we're having five hundred of our OBX T-shirts printed with a rendering of the lifesaving station and will be handing them out to attendees from our booth at the grand opening. Thank you, Fearing family, for an opportunity to let our great county shine."

Marin met her at the base of the platform and the two women embraced.

Tyde followed Lonnie to the front and the four of them locked arms. The audience broke into applause. A momentum shift toward the positive occurred inside his damaged heart. Marin held him with her can-do gaze and, for the first time, he was buoyed with a tiny hope that a promising future would outshine the tarnished past.

~

Marin recounted five weeks of frantic labor to ready the park as she stood in front of the auctioneer. The end of her summer had been a blur of construction details and housecleaning. The parking lot, boat drop-off loop, and restroom facilities had all been completed. The contractor building the climbing fort worked around the clock to put the major components in place. Seasonal park department employees planned a painting party next week to coat every surface with a gray stain to match the original Little Kinnakeet. Touches of white paint on the gingerbread fretwork would be done by the Chamber staff, which she thought was a nice gesture of support. She made a note in her organizer to bring a cold watermelon out for their enjoyment.

Maisie linked up with the Fearing men, leading them toward the spot she had selected for the bidding war. In the background, her little cottage shone like a polished stone on the edge of the famous estate, albeit no longer wanted by the landowner. With a summer's worth of salary and tips now in her bank account, she stood to stake a claim for her future. She'd have to disregard the other registered bidders by showing them the back of her paddle, an action that would bring her great pleasure.

"How's our future homeowner managing this morning?" Wade asked as they approached.

Tyde looked sturdy this morning, even amicable. He hugged her and pulled away with a slight wink.

Her stomach fluttered. "Do you mean would-be homeowner?" she asked, a quiver sitting atop her words. She pressed her paddle-holding arm against her ribs and tried to regain her composure.

The auctioneer stepped up onto his soap box and tapped the microphone.

"Going-to-be homeowner," Maisie corrected, folding her hands into prayer position and moving behind her.

Wade settled in off her bidding hand and Tyde took the other side.

"Ladies and gentlemen, Creef Auctions would like to thank each and every one of you for coming out today. I'm Joe Creef, your auctioneer and host. To start with, we'll hold the real estate portion of this auction. This will be an absolute auction of the nine hundred and thirty square foot cottage known as the gatehouse for the original Griffith estate. As stipulated, the house must be removed from the premises within thirty days of this sale. A condition of the sale, twenty percent must be paid as a deposit today, with the remainder to be paid prior to transferring the house offsite. If there are no questions, we're ready to begin the bidding."

Marin shifted her feet to open her stance, hoping to counter a slight dizzy sensation. She had a ridiculous amount of cash tucked into her fanny pack. Her future now rode on her hip. A lot of hard work and sacrifice had made that wad possible. This was her chance to make it all worthwhile. She swallowed as Wade took her elbow and raised the bidding paddle to ready position. Offering him a nervous smile, she braced. Like a breeze catching in a sail, Tyde's fingertips brushed hers and she felt released in forward motion.

"I'll start the bidding at the landowner's minimum of forty thousand," the auctioneer began. "Forty, forty, do I hear forty?" His chatty cadence crossed the yard. A short man in the front flashed his paddle and the auctioneer pointed at him.

Marin moved to counter, but Wade held her arm down.

"Forty-two now. Do I hear forty-two?"

She glanced at Wade.

He shook his head. "Wait," he whispered.

She nodded. Her heart skipped a beat when a woman down left of her made the bid to match.

"Forty-four? Now forty-four."

A finger touched her elbow and she raised her paddle. The auctioneer pointed at her and smiled. Now she had some momentum, but higher bids soon stacked like rungs on a ladder.

At fifty-two thousand dollars, the woman on the left dropped out of the bidding war. Calculating the alternating rise in bid, she could only last two or three more rounds, and then her wad would be exceeded. A wince of regret surfaced that Anna Lisa couldn't be there with her, guarding her back financially like she had promised. Too much had happened since that night, and her pledge had burned up with the artist's income and the Fearing cottage. Wade touched her elbow and she secured the fifty-two thousand bid.

Twice more she raised the paddle, but at sixty-two thousand dollars, she'd met her match. Regret now struck full force as her insufficient funds would cause her to lose the battle for her dream cottage. The auctioneer begged for any further bids, going once, then twice.

"Sixty-five," Wade called, forcing her arm up with the paddle. A swarm of murmurs ensued, but not another offered bid surfaced.

A gavel came down with thunder and Marin owned the cottage, just like that.

"Anna Lisa has your back on this… and believe me, we could have gone a lot higher," Wade admitted.

Maisie's hug swamped her next, but Marin felt Tyde's pull the strongest, like the moon over the sound. Stunned by sheer happiness, she caught his profile against the cottage's backdrop and knew she had everything she'd ever wanted, wrapped into one glorious moment. So what if it didn't come with dirt beneath it. Today, she had a house.

Chapter 22

Tyde awakened from the couch to the smell of bacon, a holiday symbol in itself. Joey stood back to him at the kitchen sink, whistling an old sailor's song. Looking only half official, the officer had his police department polo on with neatly pressed shorts.

He sat up and rubbed his eyes. "Okay, what gives?"

"Today's the big grand opening. Go grab your shower before I wake Jeremy up." He moved to the stove to turn over the bacon.

A need to retreat from the public's eye hit him between the shoulder blades. "Maybe I'll sit this one out," he replied, cradling his head in his hands.

"Out of the question… now get moving," Joey commanded. He pointed toward the bathroom and suddenly it became the apparent choice.

Tyde stood, stretching his frame. Marin came to mind halfway to the bathroom and he wondered how the day would go for her. A flush of shame came next as he realized he had barely connected with her in the past month. Maybe that was his way of letting her off the hook. Who'd want to date a homeless guy anyway? He spent the next ten minutes trying to convince himself under a steady head of steam. When he came out of the mind-clearing shower, a hot breakfast waited on the table for him. "Joey, this is beyond the call of duty." He sat down to the rousing aroma of a real meal.

The big man filled his coffee mug and hooked a smile onto his morning face. "You're going to be my assistant today, so I thought I'd pay it forward. There's nothing like a little rocket fuel to rev your engines before the start."

He raised his mug toward him as the first bite angled down the pike. Cheese melted into the scrambled eggs made him savor the sensation. He cleared his throat and decided to state his position. "I've been thinking about staying back since hubbub isn't really my thing."

"Today the Parole for Poverty event comes to a head. I have to make twenty-five 'arrests' at the grand opening before noon—and you're going to help me." Joey slipped a folded paper out of his breast pocket and showed it to him.

His name topped the list followed by his father, like they were the area's most wanted criminals. "Great, it looks like mom's been leveraging her power against us." He seized the bacon. As his hand moved toward his mouth, a silver flash came up from beneath the table's edge.

Joey clamped a pair of handcuffs over his wrist. "Now, no more talk of not coming out to help me. Don't make me have to wear the far end of that thing, or you'll have to climb over the console to get in my patrol car."

"Nice show of force, lawman. Do the rest of them get real handcuffs?"

"Only the most wanted. I'll match you to your donor when the time comes. Until then, you're stuck with me. And I plan to eat my weight in hot dogs today since they're free."

"I'll challenge you on that one, big bro." Jeremy stood in his bedroom doorway with a horrendous case of bed-head hair. "Join the dare, Tyde, if you dare keep up with a Tate."

"You're on dude," he replied, the day intensifying from lukewarm potential. He scanned the list and found the teen's name near the bottom. A smirk kept him from nibbling his bacon. "It looks like we may have a run-in later today. Don't let down your guard, Junior."

"Like you two could ever get the drop on me." He laughed and disappeared into the bathroom.

Joey slid him a knowing look as their collusion for the day of entrapment simmered over a harmless breakfast of bacon and eggs.

~

Marin held the wooden sign, which turned out to be much heavier than it looked. Two recreation employees manned the posthole diggers and churned up sleeves of packed sand off the main parking lot. How they could have forgotten the park nameplate, she couldn't begin to guess. Her eyes caressed the lettering with the hope Tyde would find it endearing.

Over by her car, the Wade's Wander nature trail sign held bits of interpretive information about the wax myrtle thicket including the Native American's use of yaupon. Everything seemed to point back to Tyde. If only he hadn't withdrawn from her lately. But today wasn't about them, it was park day. The sound-side land would be celebrated by all.

The men took possession of the sign and settled it into place. She took that as her cue to leave and headed for her car. Taking the keynote address from the seat, she grabbed a visor and slammed the door. The lock clicked and she slipped the keys into her fanny pack, disappearing into the wax myrtle thicket to enjoy her only moments of privacy for the day. Her parents were driving out from Elizabeth City with Maisie for the event, even though school started tomorrow for Northeastern High. The chipped bark path led her past a warbling mockingbird and gratitude surfaced for a moment alone with nature.

"God, please let this day be successful, with me and in spite of me, concurrently," she prayed aloud to the pine trees along the path. "Let the Fearing family experience only honor for their gift. And let the concession surprise… well let it touch Tyde deep inside, Lord. Not for my benefit, but for his own wellness. Help me care about him like you do, even if it doesn't work out to include me in the end. Amen." She spoke the words but they still stung, and when she emerged from the trail, the cart shed blurred in her vision.

A car pulled into the picnic area and she dabbed the corners of her eyes to become presentable once again. Recognizing the Chamber's SUV, she made a beeline through the play area to go assist them with setup. There, strung out like miniature sentinels, stood Hazel's lighthouses to mark the playground's perimeter. She took a deep breath and waved at the contingency.

Gwyneth held a T-shirt up in the morning breeze like a jib catching the wind. She raised her other hand and signaled her with two thumbs up.

~

Tyde had a feeling the island would tip over if any more people showed up. Joey exercised special privilege and had parked at the picnic shelter closest to the boat ramp, making his first impression truly VIP. The loop road tapered into a slope approaching the water's edge with the sand being reinforced with metal treads for better traction. He could live with that view.

"Just so you don't go getting any foolish ideas, Tyde," Joey said, tugging at the handcuff set. Jeremy made a funny face like he knew what was coming as Joey clamped the far end over his own wrist. "Now you're my deputy for the day—and my sidekick."

Tyde spotted his dad over by the set of bleachers brought in for the occasion. He pulled the joint bracelet up and pointed for Joey's benefit. "I see our first arrest. Got the cuffs?" He smiled at Jeremy and nodded toward a floating dock out hovering over the sound. The teen cut loose with a salute, leaving the arrest team to do their charity work. He scanned the playground and it simply crawled with kids. It made for a memorable scene.

"Who's up?" Joey asked as he removed the list from his pocket.

Tyde tapped his hat down over his ears. "Outlaw number two, Wade Fearing."

"Good pick, we'll go down the list in order," Joey agreed. He settled a box on his utility belt and stepped toward the grandstands, pulling Tyde along. "This is going to be a lot like the three-legged race, you know."

Tyde snickered, the merriment of the day starting to infuse his resistant hide.

~

"Welcome to Fearing Landing," Marin began. She had placed the Fearings strategically on the front row and watched Tyde absorb the moniker. She liked everything she saw. Hazel and Cordelia exchanged comments with Anna Lisa and it had an earnest feel-good to it. After finishing her introductory comments, she brought up Eli and went down to sit with her parents.

"And now to unravel the rest of the mystery surrounding the original land bequeathal," he began. "To catch everyone up, this land was deeded to Willis J. Fearing in nineteen-hundred and seven by Governor Benjamin G. Pritchard. But why, might we ask, would he be so inclined? The clue that led to my conclusion today was plucked from the staff listing for Little Kinnakeet Lifesaving Station dated eighteen ninety-nine, where both men are listed as privates on the row team. What may have transpired between the men proved to be my next mystery, for which I gained resolution when I stumbled upon the following account.

"'The schooner Robert W. Casey foundered off the North Carolina coast on August seventeenth, eighteen ninety-nine. While being driven ashore by east-northeast hurricane winds, the valiant crew of Little Kinnakeet Lifesaving Station responded with no thought of peril to their own well-being. In the captain's own words, from these "noble, gallant and heroic life-savers, there was nothing left undone."' So I pose to you what I'm hypothesizing between the lines, that Willis Fearing must have rescued the good governor-to-be during the perilous tempest. In gratitude for his very life, the rescued man, Benjamin Pritchard, endowed the hero, Willis Fearing, with the tract of land upon which we now stand.

Marin shifted to see the Fearing clan. The look on Tyde's face was priceless, like he had been exonerated for a crime he had never committed. Wade locked an arm around his shoulders, latching a generational brotherhood of watermen together. She hadn't meant to let it move her so, but the quake started in her stomach and inched up her throat. Honor ruled the day, and the Fearings stood in the middle of it. How could she not be affected? She shoved her sunglasses up the bridge of her nose to hide the tears that had begun to form.

"As to the last mystery of the day, let's get to it at long last—the racing scull." Eli shuffled toward the edge of the platform like he had somewhere to go. "Dare County Historical Society would hereby like to invite everyone to become a part of making history today. Please meet our Board members over by the cart shed and we'll have the scull brought down from the rafters. What other secrets of the past await us? Ladies and gentlemen, let's go find out."

Mayhem ensued, as a mass exodus of attendees jumped to their feet to make the journey, led by Wade Fearing. Tyde lost a half-step on him having to drag the bulk of Joey Tate along. She swished her smile to the side, knowing she was to blame for that link-up. What price she'd have to pay for that later, she could only guess.

~

Joey worked in unison with Tyde as they slid the scull over the rafters toward his father. He had looked up at the bottom of this vessel all his life and grew curious beyond belief as to what the remainder of it looked like. As his hands gripped the gunwale, decades of dust wiped free and he detected a rich tropical hardwood in the grain. Joey moved forward and he followed because of the wrist-link. At least his charity partner had two strong arms to lend him.

Wade lowered the stern end to head height. "Easy boys."

Lonnie stepped from the crowd and came beneath, making eye contact with Tyde as he stepped through. He nodded in response. The natives converged on the scull for a reconciliation of sorts, another historical marker. Something revived inside his chest and he felt more alive in the moment than he had for years. A restoration was taking place, right inside one of the oldest standing structure on the Outer Banks.

The bow peak passed and he caught sight of an imprint inside the gunwale, heightening the suspense. Joey repositioned his feet and he adjusted also, just short of the final rafter.

"Down she comes now," Wade directed like a captain. The crowd murmured and the moment the boat broke clear of the shed, applause rippled across the ranks. When they brought it out into the sunlight and toweled the woodwork off, the watercraft was a sight to behold. The crowd tightened around the cart shed ramp in anticipation.

Eli stepped in to examine the craft. "R-W-C," he read aloud. "She's from the schooner Robert W. Casey, my friends! What are the odds? They couldn't save the ship that fated day, but they saved the captain's racing scull. Why, I'm led to speculate that he must have given it to the rescue crew for their heroism that day as a token of his personal appreciation."

Applause followed and Tyde high-fived his dad with his free hand. He searched the crowd and almost missed Marin with the camera hiding her face. When it lowered, her eyes seemed ablaze. The satisfaction only lasted for an instant before regret snuffed it out. In his downward spiral after the house burned up, he'd isolated himself from her to keep her from being drawn down with him. That freefall felt out of place on such a restorative day. Now that he'd removed a precious-held gem from the rafters, he'd have to find his way back to her heart.

"And what do we find inside?" Eli accepted the first item from Wade. "A cork canteen… An oar…A small box …of snuff…Does anyone see a pattern here?"

"All this stuff floats," a young boy in front offered.

Eli pointed at him and winked. "Salvage items from the shipwreck, you're right my lad. Maybe it washed up days later, after the hurricane had moved offshore. Furthermore, the men may have elected to make a memorial out of some of the items they found on patrol. And here we are uncovering it over a hundred years later. Isn't that astounding?"

Another round of applause rose up and Tyde clapped with them, as much as Joey would allow. Cordelia Baum had stepped free of the crowd with a bossy look on her face. Talk about killing the mood. Eli tried to hush the crowd to let the old coot have her say, but it wasn't easy.

"As President of the Dare County Historical Society, I would like to invite you on a loop tour inside the cart shed at this time," she said. "Subsequently, this entrance will be cordoned off for the shed's protection, but today it belongs to the people of Dare County. Now, the name Little Kinnakeet has surfaced in relation to the men who likely brought this shed to its current position. I'd like to call your attention to the embossment in the shed's far corner, one that links it to Little Kinnakeet in both time and origin."

Tyde could finally grin at that association without feeling any recrimination, so he did. It felt nothing short of miraculous.

"But now that I see what friendship emerged between these two men, it makes me wonder about its authenticity," Cordelia posed.

The grin melted into a lump in Tyde's throat in seconds. His thoughts scattered in a thousand directions trying to figure out where she was going.

"What I'm about to say is utter speculation, but an option we hadn't considered before has just occurred to me. I don't think this shed originated from Little Kinnakeet at all. When the refurbishment of eighteen ninety-two came around, I think station number one got its shed as planned. I believe a *duplicate* structure was constructed at the governor's request and expense. And here it sits in its original location, with the same mix of sand, shell, and concrete with which the buildings at Chicamacomico were set. Then in nineteen eleven, the land around it was deeded. That's my personal hypothesis which can be added to all other plausible outcomes. But for now, let's tour the cart shed and accept it for the gift it's truly been. Who's coming with me?"

The thought of the Fearings having a duplicate shed pulsed in Tyde's veins. His father turned, regarded the scull, and lifted his gaze to the tiny building. Their eyes met and the skip in time they'd suffered vanished in a history lesson. Strong arms embraced him before he could react and he wrapped his father's shoulders, forgetting about his burnt skin and all the other scars time had dealt them.

A delicate hand touched his cheek and his mother appeared in front of him, tears streaming from beneath her sunglasses. Her eyes were healing, and now the rest of her could follow. He glanced up to locate Marin only to see her aqua top disappear into the crowd. One aspect of the healing had yet to be addressed, and the needle of awareness poked him sharply insistent.

~

With the crowd back in the grandstands, Marin took her place at the microphone to make the final presentation. At her request, Wade had joined her on the platform, seated beside a covered rack that would soon be unveiled. Anna Lisa sat with Tyde on the front row. Joey was up next, set to free his charity prisoners. But first, she would free Tyde. Free him to dream again.

"On behalf of Dare County Advocates, the Recreation Department, and the Historical Society, thank you for coming out today to experience the beauty of nature, the wonder of history, and the release of play-filled recreation. To end with recreation is a fitting tribute to the generosity of the family that made Fearing Landing possible. I'm happy to announce that I have one last surprise for us all.

"Today we not only open a public park, but we christen a cooperative venture between the Fearings and Dare County. A private company will operate a boat rental concession right here from Fearing Landing. To render the details of this venture, I've asked Wade Fearing to join me." She glanced at Tyde as she sidestepped to lend Wade the microphone. He took his hat off in slow motion like he was bracing for the news flash.

"Thanks, Ms. Evans. What a day it's turned out to be for our family—joy beyond belief. I'd like to thank my wife, Anna Lisa Golden, who had the original idea to make the land gift, as it took a heart as big as hers to get the ball rolling."

Anna Lisa blew the speaker an exaggerated kiss.

Marin dropped her gaze to her parents on the front row who were hugging. The feel-good of the moment had become infectious.

Wade shifted his stance and his handcuff jingled. "Someone once had a dream, a dream that the sound would one day be as big a draw for the Outer Banks as the oceanfront. And his dream came with boats—lots of tiny boats that drew themselves across the sound's surface by virtue of oars, paddles, and sails. Well today, I'm thrilled to announce that this dream has become reality. That dreamer is my son, Tyde Fearing, who now becomes the first statewide recipient of a North Carolina small business grant for emerging entrepreneurs."

On cue, Marin stepped down from the platform, circling around to the covered rack.

"But what's a boat concessionaire without a fleet?" Wade posed, his voice breaking over the microphone.

Marin snatched the cover off the trailer and a row of colorful new watercraft appeared racked one on top of the other on rollers for ease of unloading.

"I'll tell you what he is. He's everything he ever dreamed he could be. Welcome to Sound Strider Sports Concession where today, all rentals will be by the hour instead of half a day. How about paying a dollar for a float on Roanoke Sound, folks?"

A boisterous cheer went up. Marin lost sight of Tyde as children crowded her to see the sparkly boats. Their enthusiasm brought Wade's grant efforts to its positive conclusion. But where was her sound strider?

~

Tyde jerked at the handcuff as he raced toward the platform. "Get this thing off of me." Joey stumbled behind him as his mother rose and planted a kiss on his cheek. His blood raced and his feet couldn't wait to hit the water's edge. Eli shook his free hand as he passed by the Historical Society. Cordelia placed a hand on his shoulder while Hazel squeezed her hands into her chest, sniffing to maintain her decorum. They paused long enough to slap a set of cuffs on Jeremy, hot dog and all. Running up the steps, he almost toppled his lawman shadow.

"For the Parole for Poverty charity fundraiser," Joey stammered into the microphone, "I'll now unite the arrested with their donor. So please come on stage as your name is read and we'll unlock you—for a donation, that is. First we have Tyde Fearing. Marin Evans, will you please come get your prisoner?"

When Joey hoisted the handcuffs, it forced Tyde's hand in the air, circumventing his plan to hug Marin when she appeared. He'd have to come up with something else.

Marin slapped a folded check into Joey's free hand, which his mother immediately plucked from the policeman. The next instant, Joey freed his wrist and held out his police hat for the requisite donation. Once he'd made the payment, he picked Marin up in a fireman's carry and exited the stage.

"Wade Fearing," Joey announced next.

Anna Lisa didn't have far to travel to claim her prisoner. She handed over her bounty long enough to show affection to her long-lost husband and he complied nicely. Tyde hooked a gesture his way and descended the steps with Marin in his arms. He helped her find the ground and ran to the boat trailer. After all, they had a fleet to launch.

"Lonnie Grayton," Joey called as he continued paroling the donors from the stage.

Tyde lifted the trailer's tongue. "Dad, show me how to work this thing." When Wade grabbed hold, they shoved it back and angled for the floating dock. "Man, look at all these beautiful boats. Paddleboards, too. I'm near-bout breathless."

"This was Marin's idea," Wade replied. She found the grant proposal and I applied on your behalf. I had to co-sign on some of the paperwork for the business incorporation, so you have a partner, like it or not." They lowered the trailer by the floating dock. Wade cranked a wench that brought the first boat forward off the rollers.

"Oh, I think I'll like having a partner all right," he replied, copying the wench action on the opposite side. Marin put her hands on the stern as it rolled off and they carried the red boat down to the sound. "Water Strider Two," he read off the bow.

Marin gave a little grin. "Your mother's handiwork," she replied with a shrug of her shoulders.

He came up with a handful of water and gave her a flirting splash.

She did the adult thing and stuck her tongue out at him. "The oars are in the gear box on back. I'll get them and let you help Wade."

Happiness rushed through him at the thought of touching another boat. This one was painted blue. In seconds he stood beside his dad, watching a deferred dream come true.

~

Possibly the longest day of her life, Marin had nothing to eat but hot dogs, but it still seemed like she floated on a cloud. Nothing had broken, no one had been hurt, and she even had a new T-shirt with her favorite park on the front. She sat on the end of the floating dock while Tyde cradled the last boat with his father, lowering it onto the top rack. The sun tempted to touch the horizon over the sound and the park gates had been officially closed for the first time. Anna Lisa had departed to make a bank run with all the charity donations. Wade mentioned something about Jimbo's restaurant and soon took off in his car. Finally, they were on the edge of the Fearing exclusion all alone.

A movement caught her eye and she looked up to see the original Water Strider floating out toward her empty. Tyde came down the dock with two oars crossed in front of him.

She'd been waiting days for this moment with him, so why didn't the knot in the bottom of her stomach untie?

He knelt and looked at her with a gleam in his eyes. "Once upon a time there was an islander who didn't care for the oceanfront," he said, like he was quoting a fairy tale. He extended an oar and tilted his head. "Would a fair maiden like you want to put to sea with a man like that?" The question seemed to float in the air like a line cast above the waters.

"With the Good Lord as my witness, I would indeed," she replied, accepting the oar he offered. She stepped down into the familiar boat and took her half of the stern bench.

Tyde eased into the vessel and cast it away from the dock with a shove. Without hesitation, he took his seat beside her. "Where to now?" he asked, his voice turning husky.

She leaned in to close the gap and her motion melded into a kiss under his hat brim, the one she'd been hoping for all day. The boat rocked with the weight displacement, but he corrected the off-centered happenstance with a valiant shift toward the middle. She gave up her space and slid onto his lap as he took the first oar stroke into their future. On the water again at last, only togetherness mattered. And their little boat proved highly seaworthy as its bow prodded the setting sun at the far end of Roanoke Sound.

Epilogue

With the clock ticking down before the vow renewal ceremony, Marin turned into the lane of her gatehouse under the stress of running late. She fidgeted with the lace neckline with the hope it would stay up on her tanned shoulders. A glance at Maisie in the passenger seat revealed she had similar trouble as her crisscross bodice gaped open. Anna Lisa had orchestrated these dresses to be camera-friendly, but somehow managed to forget one factor—wear-ability.

"Did I mention Jeremy registered for classes at College of the Albemarle?" Maisie asked. "He's rooming with a cousin in town, but Mom says he can study at our house anytime."

She drove in behind the cottage, which now sat jacked onto massive beams designed to lend stability during transport. The crane would arrive tomorrow and hoist it onto the barge. When it launched across Roanoke Sound to nestle the structure into the Fearing exclusion, it would become a double-dream come true.

The engagement ring on her finger held that promise.

With one final glance in the rearview mirror, she checked the clock and panicked. "We have to run, sis." She pulled a tendril loose on each side of her fancy up-do and exited in not-so-lady-like fashion, her satiny skirts hitched on her hips. It was not her style to be late.

Maisie ran ahead looking like a woodland fairy. Jeremy met her in the side yard and assisted her toward the waterfront with a genial laugh.

As Marin cleared the front corner of the house, a storybook vision unfolded, with tiny lights entwined around tulle that festooned the barge for the vow renewal ceremony. Her breath caught as she watched the lights shimmer off the water all around the floating platform. Music played and she spotted a violinist by the crepe myrtle tree. Rows of chairs in the front yard held friends and family, including her mom and dad. Maisie slowed at the gang plank, raised her chin in regal charm, and walked aboard with Jeremy's escort.

Next, Anna Lisa paired with Wade and they stepped onto the plank arm-in-arm. Instead of centering themselves under the lighted arch, they shifted to the right side and turned around as though anticipating company. *How odd.*

Tyde appeared at the far end of the plank wearing a suit that made him look like something out of a magazine. He beckoned to her with a crook of his finger.

Marin's mouth wicked dry. She approached between the rows into a makeshift aisle and froze. Her skin pricked with partial awareness like something treasured lay just beyond her reach. To her right, the painting of Tyde posed by the porch railing sat on a tall easel, a white bow decorating its corner. She sensed the gift had been intended for her. *What was going on?*

When her mother stood and faced her, the rest of the attendees followed suit. The string music shifted to a traditional bridal march. Eli slipped from his chair, stepped beside her, and cradled her elbow with his time-worn hand. Knees trembling, she managed first one step and then another. When she arrived along the front row, her mother handed her a ribbon-wrapped bouquet of wispy sea lavender trimmed with yaupon sprigs. Her father nodded toward the barge and gave her a sly wink of approval.

Marin's disbelief ebbed. In steps, her satiny shoes toed the plank's edge. Eli halted, squeezed her arm, and dropped back to his seat. The sound waters lapped against the barge and blended with the violin music. Almost full, the moon dripped indirect light from above, which cast a liquid sheen over the entire scene. At the end of her gaze, there stood Tyde.

"Come on out," he beckoned, his voice saturated with affection.

Only one outcome remained. Her foot hit the plank under surrender's bidding as Tyde's face lit in anticipation. Of course, she would have to leave the land now. After all, she loved a waterman. Where the plank ended, he took her hand. The sway of the barge carried her away.

<u>OTHER BOOKS BY CINDY M. AMOS</u>

LANDSCAPES OF MERCY SERIES

Book One   *Redeeming River Rancher*

Book Two   *Saving Bicycle Man*

9 781944 203771